Blood on the Bayou

About Heather Graham

Heather Graham has been writing for many years and actually has published nearly 200 titles. So, for this page, we'll concentrate on the Krewe of Hunters.

They include:

Phantom Evil
Heart of Evil
Sacred Evil
The Evil Inside
The Unseen
The Unholy
The Unspoken
The Uninvited
The Night is Watching
The Night is Alive
The Night is Forever
The Cursed
The Hexed
The Betrayed
The Silenced
The Forgotten
The Hidden

Actually, though, Adam Harrison—responsible for putting the Krewe together, first appeared in a book called Haunted. He also appeared in Nightwalker and has walk-ons in a few other books. For more ghostly novels, readers might enjoy the Flynn Brothers Trilogy—Deadly Night, Deadly Harvest, and Deadly

Gift, or the Key West Trilogy—Ghost Moon, Ghost Shadow, and Ghost Night.

The Vampire Series (now under Heather Graham/ previously Shannon Drake) Beneath a Blood Red Moon, When Darkness Falls, Deep Midnight, Realm of Shadows, The Awakening, Dead by Dusk, Blood Red, Kiss of Darkness, and From Dust to Dust.

For more info, please visit her web page, http://www.theoriginalheathergraham.com or stop by on Facebook.

Blood on the Bayou

A Cafferty & Quinn Novella

By Heather Graham

1001 Dark Nights

EVIL EYE
CONCEPTS

Blood on the Bayou
A Cafferty & Quinn Novella
Copyright 2016 Heather Graham Pozzessere
ISBN: 978-1-942299-51-6

Foreword: Copyright 2014 M. J. Rose

Published by Evil Eye Concepts, Incorporated

Dear Reader,

I have an absolute love for the City of New Orleans and a great deal of Southern Louisiana. I'm not from there—I am a Floridian from start to finish. But, when I was very young, I went on business trip to the city with my dad. No, we did not walk down Bourbon Street. He took me to the zoo, showed me the beautiful architecture and the eerie beauty of the cemeteries. I was smitten.

Every year since Katrina, friends have helped me put on Writers for New Orleans—a writers' conference at cost; at first, it was just to bring people back into an empty city.

Now, it's because we can't seem to stop!

Being in love with the city, it's where I chose a shop for Danni Cafferty. The first Cafferty and Quinn book, Let the Dead Sleep, 2013, introduces Cafferty and Quinn and the Cheshire Cat, her shop on Royal Street. In that first book, Danni loses her father, a fascinating old Highlander she has adored. (Shades of author intrusion there!)

And she finds out just what kind of legacy he has left her.

Let the Dead Sleep was followed by Waking the Dead. (Hey! They slept long enough.) And, next, Let the Dead Play On. (All available through Mira Books!)

The books are near and dear to me, like the City of New Orleans. I can walk down Royal Street and see my imaginary shop there—right around the Rodrique studios (I love the Blue Dog!) and one of my favorite places ever to shop—Fifi Mahoney's. They have a salon, and they also sell some of the most artistic and amazing wigs to be found anywhere, along with funky jewelry and cool cosmetics.

I can imagine Danni and Quinn moving about the city; I know how they feel about tourists, and what they really like to do with their down time.

This year, I'll be coming out with a new series in Spring, straight suspense, revolving around a New York City FBI agent and a young woman working with criminal psychology—who also happens to be part owner of a pre-Civil War Irish pub. Kieran's family has a checkered past—towing the line between her brothers and the law is often a tricky task, and despite herself, she's suddenly involved in diamond heists about the city that suddenly begin to end with murder.

But, that's for the future.

Now, I hope you'll enjoy this Cafferty and Quinn novella—they're like old friends to me now, so I know I'll be working with them again.

One Thousand And One Dark Nights

Once upon a time, in the future...

*I was a student fascinated with stories and learning.
I studied philosophy, poetry, history, the occult, and
the art and science of love and magic. I had a vast
library at my father's home and collected thousands
of volumes of fantastic tales.*

*I learned all about ancient races and bygone
times. About myths and legends and dreams of all
people through the millennium. And the more I read
the stronger my imagination grew until I discovered
that I was able to travel into the stories... to actually
become part of them.*

*I wish I could say that I listened to my teacher
and respected my gift, as I ought to have. If I had, I
would not be telling you this tale now.
But I was foolhardy and confused, showing off
with bravery.*

*One afternoon, curious about the myth of the
Arabian Nights, I traveled back to ancient Persia to
see for myself if it was true that every day Shahryar
(Persian: شهریار, "king") married a new virgin, and then
sent yesterday's wife to be beheaded. It was written
and I had read, that by the time he met Scheherazade,
the vizier's daughter, he'd killed one thousand
women.*

Something went wrong with my efforts. I arrived in the midst of the story and somehow exchanged places with Scheherazade – a phenomena that had never occurred before and that still to this day, I cannot explain.

Now I am trapped in that ancient past. I have taken on Scheherazade's life and the only way I can protect myself and stay alive is to do what she did to protect herself and stay alive.

Every night the King calls for me and listens as I spin tales. And when the evening ends and dawn breaks, I stop at a point that leaves him breathless and yearning for more. And so the King spares my life for one more day, so that he might hear the rest of my dark tale.

As soon as I finish a story... I begin a new one... like the one that you, dear reader, have before you now.

Prologue

So far David Fagin was pleased.

"We have a few legends around here," he said to the group. "The Honey Swamp monster being one. It's said that he lives side by side with the *rougarou*."

He smiled at two of the young women in front of the group who were clad in heavy coats and huddling together.

"Every good swamp has a monster," he said. "Any of you seen *The Creature from the Black Lagoon*? Maybe not. It's a classic. But, hey, there's always Netflix. Anyway, it was a 1954 black and white film. Horrible special effects compared to what we see today, but kind of cool when you think about the poor stunt man in that rubber suit. It's your typical swamp monster. Big, scaly, out to kidnap beautiful young women and do in the handsome young men out to save them. The *rougarou*, he's different, and he's partial to this area."

"What's that word again?" someone asked.

"Rougarou." And he was careful to sound it out phonetically.

Ru-ga-ru. "Some say he's French. Others make him part Native American. He's the size of a man, but stronger. Some compare him to the Wendigo of certain local tribes. Now the Wendigo's name has been translated to mean *cannibal,* and by some to mean *the evil spirit that devours mankind.* Most agree the name derives from the French, *loup-garou,* wolf-man. The creature is usually seen as bipedal, with the head of a wolf. Sometimes, he's seen with other monstrous heads."

Though he and Julian Henri had been in business for several years, this was their first time doing the Bayou Night Myth and Legends Tour. Even Mother Nature had cooperated. No snow on the ground, or even in the air, but the night still brisk. Southern Louisiana seldom received snow, and when it did fall it didn't stay long on the ground. Out on the water, though, the cold rose like a mist, embracing the bayou and making everything seem all the more dark, chilling, and menacing.

Insects serenaded the gathering. An owl hooted beneath a full moon. Every now and then came the splash of a gator sliding down a mud bank into the water. Even the sounds of Highway 90 in the distance added to the eerie feel.

Julian's family had long owned property and few people knew the swamp better. Both of his parents had passed away during the years he'd been at college. Once he returned, everyone had urged him to sell. Byron Grayson, the realtor, had advised keeping swampland was ridiculous. He'd be happy to take it off Julian's hands. Victoria Miller, owner of another tour business, had offered Julian even more money for the property. Victoria's significant other, Gene Andre, the son of an old Cajun family himself, had urged her to buy both the land and the business. But Julian had determined that he and David could make a real success of it.

Now David was convinced that they could.

So far, on their first outing, not a hitch, and people seemed to be loving it.

David, like Julian, also hailed from the low country, which added a bit of authenticity to everything they planned to do on this tour. Though they often faked their Cajun accents. Four years at Harvard had nearly caused David to "pahk his kah." And Julian's stint at NYU in the theater department had seen to it that he could switch into a Bronx drawl just as quickly as he could spit out his hometown *patois*.

They'd returned home from their respective universities four years ago, had a chance meeting at a favorite café on Magazine Street, then two years ago ventured into the tourist business. They'd started out doing history tours in the French Quarter, then added plantation visits. A day on the bayou had been next, and now they'd moved to the Night Myths and Legends Tour by lamplight.

As always, when they started a new tour, they led the first few themselves and played up their Cajun heritage. Thanks to reality TV, people pretty much expected them to be toothless and illiterate. But breaking stereotypes was fun.

Their pontoon boat afforded a seat for the captain and the tour guide. Tonight Julian served as captain and David the guide.

"This swamp has often been a hideout place for pirates, smugglers, and outlaws," David said. "The unwary who seek shelter here. Those who don't respect the dangers because they're in trouble. Legend has it that, from time to time, the *rougarou* has happened upon those who hid in the swamp. You have to be real careful here."

A nearby alligator slid into the water.

One of the young women in front let out a short scream and jumped in her seat.

"That's probably old Meg," he said. "She's an irritable bag. Been around a long time and just isn't fond of tourists."

"Is a gator as scary as that *rougarou* thing?" a man in back called out.

"Few things are as scary as the *rougarou*," David said. "Remember, this region was largely French and the French were good Catholics. You know how it goes that if you're bitten by a werewolf in the light of the full moon, you become one."

Nervous giggling greeted his words.

"Down here, we've always mixed our monsters with religion. Part of the legend has it that the *rougarou* could enter the soul of a man who didn't follow the traditions of Lent. That was a time of trying hard to be good and behave, with kindness and brotherhood toward your fellow man. Bad guys have bad things happen. Good guys get good. And, you see, if such a man had his soul stolen by the *rougarou*, he would kill all the decent men."

"So the bad guy became badder and the good guys paid?" a teenager asked him. "Maybe it's cool being the *rougarou*."

"Not really. Because the good guys would hunt down the *rougarou*, bash his head and slice his throat," David said. "Then they cut off his head and chop out his heart." He smiled. "So, *rougarou*, watch out."

He allowed his story to sink in before telling them more about their surroundings.

"A swamp is defined as low-lying, uncultivated ground where water collects. A bayou is a body of water lying in flat lowland, an offshoot of a slow moving river or marshy lake or wetland. It's low water with all kinds of creatures and trees, with civilization far away. But not so far anymore, as you can almost see the lights of the highway from here."

He grinned.

"1756 to 1763 are the important years. The English and French are fighting. The French from Acadia, in what is now Canada, came south to escape persecution from the English. Cajun culture comes from that time. French fur traders first came to this area in the late 1690s, and it was the French who founded New Orleans in 1718. *Nouvelle Orleans.*"

"*Viva la France,*" one of the teens shouted.

David smiled. "Absolutely. However, the city and surrounding areas were ceded to the Spanish as a secret provision of the Treaty of Fontainebleau after the Seven Years' War. It took a long time for the Spanish to gain any kind of control, and the flavor of the city remained French, though slowly mixing with Spanish. Then fires ravaged the city. When the area was rebuilt it all became Spanish."

"Bravo Spain!" another said.

"Again, absolutely," David said. "But in 1801, another treaty gave it all back to the French. By then the Americans had arrived with permission to use the ports. I'm telling you all this to explain the mix of cultures and culture clash. The French had their *rougarou*. When the Americans came, they added the Anglo church, and though the fear of witches had died out, it was resurrected here. We already had our African-Caribbean voodoo thing going. So we just added all the new stuff in to our own legends."

He pointed out in the dark.

"Just to the right, ahead, is the site where the Good Witch of Honey Swamp lived in the early 1800s. Her father had been a Scottish sailor, her mother a voodoo queen. She cured people, and it was claimed she could control the weather."

He shifted everyone's attention in another direction with a hand gesture.

"Back over there you'll see some old houses built up by the bayou. They look close, but they're about a mile apart. They've been there all these years, owned first by the rich, and now by us working stiffs. Our good captain, Julian Henri, lives up there."

"A working stiff, I assure you," Julian called out.

Laughter rose among the passengers.

Julian pointed far to the left. "Right over there, friends, that old shack on the water is my place. I grew up around here as an only child. Alligators were my pets."

Of course, not a word of it was true. But it sounded great.

David started to speak, then paused, a bit puzzled. He could have sworn he saw lights flashing by Julian's place. Though he owned it, Julian did not live there. He stayed in the French Quarter, where they kept their offices. He did keep a few lights on in the place, but they didn't flash. Maybe it had been a trick of the moon.

"Alligator for a pet," someone said. "Really?"

"Not much to cuddle with at night," Julian teased.

"It's so creepy out here," one of the young women in front said. "Weren't you always scared?"

"When you grow up out here, you don't think about it," Julian explained. "It's just home."

"Even with old *rougarous* and witches and voodoo and whatever else?" someone asked.

"Now that's the thing. When you're from here, you're protected."

Then Julian shrugged at David, turning the group back over to him.

David took the cue and said, "Some say that the Good Witch of Honey Swamp offended a powerful slaveholder who called himself Count D'Oro. He owned one of the houses, like Julian's, on the water. The Good Witch had no interest in becoming his mistress or performing her magic for him. So one night the Good Witch of Honey Swamp was dragged from her home, tied to a tree, and burned alive. She made it rain, and the rain kept putting out the fire. But finally, the flames consumed her. As she died she cursed the count and all who knew him. It's said that her curse backfired. Count D'Oro turned into a *rougarou* and slaughtered dozens of people before he was caught, before he had his head bashed in and his throat ripped out, before being tied to a stake and burned to nothing but ash. They still say if the witch's curse is repeated, the soul of D'Oro will come back. And the *rougarou* will roam the swamp once again."

"What were the witch's words?" a teen asked.

A shrill scream pierced the night.

From one of the young women toward the front of the boat.

For a moment, it seemed that David's heart stopped. Had they been moving too close to shore? Was another alligator aiming toward the pontoon boat?

"The *rougarou*," the young woman screeched, moving from her seat.

"Careful," he warned.

The pontoon boat shouldn't flip, but with such a sudden shift of weight he wasn't sure. "Please, please. What is it? If you saw something in the trees—"

"No," the young woman cried, looking over at him with huge eyes. "Blood. There's blood on the bayou and a man. He's dead."

David carefully moved to her side of the boat.

They were close to the shore.

And he saw it.

A dead man.

Feet still tangled in the grass, head battered, blood dripping.

"*Rougarou*," someone else shouted. "They're moving in the trees."

And there was someone out there.

Gone in a flash, racing away, thrashing through the underbrush.

Rougarou? No way. They weren't real.

Not like the corpse.

And the blood on the bayou.

Chapter 1

Michael Quinn heard the hysterical crying the minute he entered the police station. The young woman creating the commotion was inside Detective Jake Larue's office. Someone else was trying to soothe her while not becoming hysterical herself.

"This one is right up your alley," Larue told him as he approached.

"My alley?"

"That young woman is certain she saw a *rougarou*. She was on a bayou tour in Honey Swamp last night."

He smiled. No kid grew up in Southern Louisiana without hearing about the *rougarou*. Every region of the world had their own particular brand of monster. The *rougarou* belonged to the Cajun region of Southern Louisiana, stretching right into the city.

"Honey Swamp?" he asked. "Doesn't a problem in that area go to the Pearl River police?"

"Yep," Larue said. "But she's here because she believes the *rougarou* followed her home, showing up in the window of her hotel last night."

He arched a brow at the ridiculousness of the statement.

"I'm assuming there's more."

"A dead man in the swamp. Head bashed in, throat ripped."

Which grabbed his attention.

"I want you to talk to them," Larue said. "I told them that you're a *rougarou* expert and that you'll get to the bottom of things. They were out on some night ghost tour in the bayou and their boat came upon the dead man. Right now, she's so hysterical that she's not making sense. But you *rougarou* experts are used to dealing with that."

He shook his head at Larue's sarcasm. He was no more a *rougarou* expert than someone was a ghost expert. Once upon a time, he'd worked with Larue as partners in the NYPD. Before that, Quinn's life had been anything but normal. He'd actually been a pretty horrible person, not as in deadly or criminal, but as in vain and egotistical. His prowess in sports had led to excess, which eventually led to him being declared legally dead.

Which changed everything.

While clinically dead, he'd seen a strange personage, who told him it was time to turn around. An angel? Maybe. But the experience had led him to the military, then the police—and then to Angus Cafferty. When Angus died, neglecting to tell his own child, Danni, what he really did on and during many of his buying trips, Quinn had brought her up to speed. It hadn't been easy. She'd not believed anything he'd said, nor had she much liked him.

In fact, she'd loathed him.

He'd never imagined how hard it would be to make her believe that all things in life were not what they seemed. But most legends had their roots in truth. She'd both grown up with Angus and wanted to believe that the world was filled with good. She was, however, her father's daughter. So when she finally came around to realizing what they were sometimes up against, she'd been brilliant.

And still exquisite.

Five-feet-nine-inches of willowy perfection, vitality, and intelligence. A mane of sleek auburn hair and the kind of blue eyes that seemed endless and could steal a man's soul. He always smiled when he thought of their rocky beginning.

She was both stubborn and opinionated.

But he couldn't imagine life without her.

His smile widened before noticing his friend's stare. Larue was studying him. When they'd been partners, Larue had known Quinn had something of an extra sense, and Larue wasn't the kind to fight, deny, or question it. In fact, Larue didn't want to know what lurked beneath the surface. He just wanted whatever bad was happening to stop. So he tended to bring Quinn in on the unusual stuff, which allowed Quinn to be both a private investigator and have the police on his side.

"You can help?" Larue asked.

"How long have we both lived around here?" he asked Larue.

"Lifetimes."

"And have you ever seen a *rougarou*?"

"Look, I'm not you," Larue said. "I don't have the gift, or whatever it is. Anyway, the Pearl River guys are working the murder. Two fellows I know fairly well, Hayden Beauchamp and Dirk Deerfield. Good detectives. Beauchamp called me this morning. The tour directors and the guests on the boat were all out of New Orleans. I've got a car ready to head out so you can meet with them and see the murder site, if you think you can help."

He pointed at his old friend. "Say what you will, but we've heard the legends for years on a *rougarou.*"

"I get it. That's why you're going to need to be on this," Larue softly said. "Did you hear what I said? Head bashed in, throat ripped out. That's only happened once before that I know about, and, of course, you know about it too."

Quinn winced and nodded.

He didn't believe that a *rougarou* had wandered into the French Quarter to jump around the guests' windows. But he did remember the murders that had taken place out at Honey Swamp when they'd been kids.

"There's more," Larue said.

He waited.

Larue pointed to the two women in his office. "There were drops of blood on the balcony where they're staying. So far, we know it's human and that's about it. We have it as a top priority, but we don't have any DNA results back yet. It all sounded like a prank when they walked in here. I don't have your ability with the strange or whatever, but I do have a cop's sixth sense. And something tells me that this is going to get worse, and weirder, before it's all over. Will you talk to these women for me, please, Quinn? God help us, we might have been kids back then, and it's not like we don't still have our fair share of pretty awful crime, but this could be like last time."

And he knew what that meant.

Serial killings.

"We have to jump on this," Larue said. "Or the whole damned bayou, and maybe this town itself, will run red with blood again."

* * * *

"I'm opening up," Danni Cafferty called to her friend Billie McDougal.

She walked across the first floor of the old house at the corner of Royal Street that she'd inherited from her father, unlocking the door of the shop portion and flipping over the OPEN sign.

She was smiling.

It was going to be an exceptionally good Friday because she couldn't wait for the night.

They, meaning herself, Quinn, Bo Ray Thompkins, Billie, Father Ryan and Natasha, also know as Mistress LaBelle, were going to get together as soon as they all closed up for the day. Also, it was going to be a night when they could bundle up a bit. New Orleans was actually chilly in January. Even the mules drawing the carriages filled with tourists seemed to enjoy the respite from the heat, clopping down the streets with what seemed like a hop in their steps.

They were planning an evening of great food and music. Not necessarily an all-nighter, which was easily possible in a city that never slept. Her shop, the Cheshire Cat, would be open tomorrow, a Saturday, but not until eleven. And Quinn, a might-have-been-guitar-player, was scheduled to sit in with friends down at a bar on Chartres Street. She loved when he played. He wasn't quite as good as many of their friends, who spent just about all of their waking hours playing their guitars. But he could have been if that'd been his goal. He was a natural and he loved it.

And she loved Quinn.

Go figure. When he first strutted into her life she'd thought him an arrogant hunk. She'd hated the fact that Angus Cafferty working with Quinn had been a secret her father had kept from her.

But things were different now.

And it wasn't just physical, though he was near the perfect man, lean of muscle, all six-four of him. It was that she knew that even when he'd been hero-worshipped by kids as a star athlete, he might have been oblivious but never cruel. She'd thought him the biggest ass the world had ever known when they first met. But eventually, she learned, after her father's death and through a difficult and deadly case involving the theft of a special statue, that he was far from it. He'd changed and become a man with a dedication to the world and those around them.

A person even her father had trusted.

Sure, the beginning hadn't been easy, and life still made things a challenge between them. But there was something that made the challenges worth it, and sleeping with him every night certainly helped ease away the day's dilemmas.

"I'm ready," Billie called to her, grinning.

His words trilled.

Billie had come to America with her father from Scotland. And though he'd been in the States for years, his rich Scottish burr hadn't faded. Tall and gaunt with a thick thatch of white hair, Billie could have easily stood in for Riff Raff in a performance of *The Rocky Horror Picture Show*. He was as dear to her as a man could be, her self-appointed guardian after her father's death, and the one who, with Quinn, had finally allowed her to see just what her father had really *collected* through the years.

"I'll be bringing me pipes," Billie assured. "And don't roll your eyes at me, lass. I'll just see if I can't be part of one or two songs."

"I love it when you play your pipes," Danni said. "It's just that the bar is small and bagpipes are loud. But it's great to have them."

Billie laughed. "Hey, now. I just want you to know, Miss Danni Cafferty, I made good money in me younger years standing on the streets with me hat out. You should have seen the folks throwing bills in it when I played."

"Maybe they were paying you to stop," Danni teased.

"Ah, lass."

"Kidding, Billie. I love it when you play."

"Here's hoping Quinn does make it back," he said, "and that he's not starting into some fresh trouble with Detective Larue. I'm looking forward to some fun times this evening."

"Don't worry. Quinn said he'd be back in plenty of time, and we'll head right out at closing."

The front door opened quickly and a tall man entered.

Who she recognized.

David Fagin.

She greeted him, curious because of his anxious manner.

David was an old friend. They'd gone to high school together, one of those magnet schools for the arts. She'd been in visual art and David had focused on theater. They'd bumped into each other a few times over the last three or four years, and he'd come to her father's funeral. They'd talked about the changes in their lives, their plans and dreams, and she recalled how he'd been excited about his business ventures. She'd told him that she was happy too, still working as an artist, running her father's shop.

David had dropped by a dozen times, but today he seemed to not be on a buying excursion.

"Danni, I need your help."

Billie stepped up beside her, ready to listen to whatever it was their visitor was about to say. She noticed how David shifted on his feet and kept looking around, as if someone were after him.

"Danni, I've heard... There are rumors. We're talking a life or death situation." His eyes focused on hers. "My life."

She swallowed hard and felt a sense of dread. She wanted to push David back out the door and pretend he'd never come. Every once in a while it was still difficult to reconcile all that had happened in the last several years. She'd thought her father the most wonderful man in the world. Tall, sturdy, and gruff, the perfect Highlander with his rich accent, booming voice, strength, and kindness. He'd traveled the world. On buying trips. Only after his death had she learned that they had been anything but.

Oh yes, Angus Cafferty had been a collector.

At the Cheshire Cat they sold local art, jewelry, clothing, and some more unusual items. Angus had especially loved unique pieces, one-of-a-kind carved masks, Egyptian trinkets, religious artifacts, custom items. One of the display cases had been created from an authentic Egyptian sarcophagus. A display in the left window featured a Victorian coffin, a turn-of-the-century mannequin, and a 19th century vampire hunting kit. The right window held local lore. A stunning display from the so-called Count D'Oro, an 18th century aristocrat who murdered numerous young women and dumped their bodies in the swamp. Among them, a beautiful, young witch who had cursed him at her death. Legend noted that he'd been a cruel man whose soul had been consumed by the devil, and only when he'd been caught by vigilantes and then burned alive in the swamp himself had his evil been laid to rest.

But Angus had also acquired the *dangerous*.

Items best described as having evil upon them.

And as the inheritor of the business, she now was their owner.

"Okay, David, let's have a chat," she said.

A nod to Billie and he understood to cover the store. She led David through the shop, past her studio, and opened the kitchen door where Wolf, Quinn's giant mixed breed dog, bounded toward her, then let out a loud woof at the sight of a stranger.

"He's a friend," she told the dog, then turned to David. "Don't be afraid of Wolf. He's a good dog. If he thought Quinn or I were in danger he'd rip into someone like hell on wheels, but as soon as he knows you're a friend he's like a puppy."

"Hey, Wolf," David said. It seemed like there was a catch in his throat when he said the dog's name.

"Sit, please." She motioned to the small breakfast nook. "Coffee?"

"In lieu of a morning shot of whiskey? Sure."

He took a seat as indicated but still looked jittery enough to shoot through the ceiling.

Danni poured coffee as David surveyed the kitchen.

"I got a note," he said.

She laid two cups of coffee on the kitchen table and sat to join him.

His fingers drummed nervously. He looked at her, his dark eyes haunted and serious. "From the *rougarou*."

She studied him and could tell he was serious. Quinn was a licensed private investigator. And, apparently, during the years she'd been blissfully naïve, her father, and the shop, had gained a certain hush-hush following, a place where people turned when they needed help with strange, life-threatening events. She wished Quinn was here now. But Detective Larue had called him that morning and he'd gone in to help with whatever Jake wanted. He wouldn't be back until early evening.

"The *rougarou* killed a man last night, Danni. Killed him horribly, about a minute before we reached him. There was still blood in the water. His head was bashed in, skull cracked like an egg, throat torn out." He drew a deep breath. "Bitten out. By savage teeth."

Her heart skipped a beat at the horror, and she could only imagine the sight he'd seen.

"The *rougarou*?" she asked.

Her window display dealt with the *rougarou*, a monster said to consume the souls of the evil and turn them into killing machines.

David curled his hands around his mug, seemingly baffled and defeated. "I just heard myself. I can't believe what I said.

And I'm from that damned swamp. I grew up along the Pearl River. Yeah, we base the business here in the city, and my apartment now is just off Esplanade on Bourbon, but I know that swamp. I've trapped gators, caught catfish as a summer job, worked crawfish nets. I know the bayou."

She'd always liked David. He'd majored in theater, but she'd always thought he might have turned into a playwright. He loved to tell stories. Had a flair for the dramatic, which he'd used to make a good living with the tour company he'd started with Julian Henri. There, his love of local lore and dramatic talents had combined perfectly. She knew that he and Julian had accumulated raves from almost every online travel site.

"*Rougarou*. I think the thing is real," he muttered. "I didn't at first. I mean, it was all going so well. The *rougarou* was a legend told to scare kids, to make us be safe, to make us behave. All the stories about the Good Witch and Count D'Oro. They're just that. Stories. Last night, the tour boat was full and we were going to make some serious money. We're booked for weeks to come. But I don't know now. I've put the tours on hold and returned the fees paid. We were telling the tales, talking about the area, working the group, and then we found a dead man."

She'd not seen nor heard any of the local news for the day. Most of the time Billie or Bo Ray managed the shop. She was there often, but thanks to them she could focus more on her studio and be with Quinn. More time to deal with problems just like this one since, after all, she had inherited the Cheshire Cat and all that came with it. Now she realized that Jake Larue had probably called Quinn because of the murder—even if it had occurred way out in Honey Swamp.

"David, you do understand that whoever killed this man may have been aware of our local legends and just used one to their advantage."

She could barely remember the details of when the last

bayou murders had taken place. Understandable, given she was only six. But it was as if history was repeating itself. History from long ago.

And from not so long ago.

He looked at her, his thoughts apparently running parallel with hers. "You remember, don't you? It was the same thing. Those young women out in the swamp. Three of them. And they never did catch the killer. They blamed it on the *rougarou*. The local people did, anyway. The press dubbed him the Wolfman Killer because of what happened to the throats. That was twenty years ago. Then the killing stopped. And now?" His voice carried anguish. "What else could it be?"

"There are still many logical reasons why this happened, David. Even in the way it did. There are still the normal motives for murder. Someone was furious. Someone wanted to get even. Jealousy, hatred, greed. And this someone knows the legend, as we do, and thought that killing like that would cause everyone to get scared and shake the police off the right track. Yes, this is truly horrible, but I'm still confused. You said that the *rougarou* sent you a note?" She tried to smile and ease his sense of fear. "This is the first time I've ever heard that the *rougarou* liked to write."

David's fear wasn't eased, nor was he amused, and he glared at her. "In the mud, Danni. He wrote in the mud. Near the dock. Julian brought the people and our boat back in. I went with the police. But when they brought me back in I saw it by the floodlights we keep burning by the dock. There were letters, weird letters, like a kid had written them."

"What did they say?"

"'I'm coming for you.'"

David's voice was just a sliver of sound on the air.

"The area had been pretty trampled by then. People were really freaked out. They couldn't wait to get back on the bus.

The police had to interview them all." He tightened his hold and dropped his gaze to his mug. "The cops didn't see what I saw, Danni. And before I could tell them to stop, they walked all over the letters, erasing every last one."

"David, that message could have been for anyone. You said there were twenty or so people on the tour. And it might have been innocent, like someone's friend trying to say that they'd be there to pick them up instead of them coming back into town."

"You don't get it, Danni."

He thrust a finger into his chest.

"My name was there. In the mud. It said, 'David, I'm coming for you.'"

Chapter 2

"I know it was a monster."

Jane Eagle appeared to be the younger of the two women seated in Larue's office—and the most hysterical.

"Okay," Quinn said gravely, not disputing her. He turned to her friend and travel companion, Lana Adair, and asked, "Did you see the monster?"

Lana tossed Jane a guilty expression, as if she hated telling the truth. "I didn't see him. Not in the swamp. But I did see the dead man. His head was...there was blood in the water and...white stuff. I mean the poor fellow's brains. Oh, God."

"Did you see the monster at your balcony window?" Quinn asked.

Lana shook her head, glancing sadly at Jane again. "I did see what looked like bloody prints of some kind. We didn't even call the police. We left and got a cab because we didn't know where we were going and asked for the closest police station. Detective Larue sent some men out right away, and he told us it was blood."

"The guy on the boat wasn't lying," Jane said. "It was a monster. A *rougarou*. That's what he was talking about. And he was so good, so knowledgeable. He was great. Until—"

"The body in the bayou. And for all that blood and stuff to

be in the water, it had to just have happened," Lana said.

"The guide didn't freak out. I think his friend did a little. Or his partner. The captain. His name was Julian. After the lady saw the body and yelled, he turned white. Then the guide—"

"David," Jane said. "Cute. Nice."

"He was pretty competent," Lana said. "He got on some kind of radio and called the police. They came in a boat. David, yeah. David, that's his name. Anyway, he got on the cop boat and the captain brought us back to the dock to be questioned."

"We were all freaked out on the bus back to the city," Jane said. "We had drinks."

"Lots of them," Lana added.

"Oh, we don't usually," Jane said. "I mean, yeah, it's New Orleans, but we're not big drinkers. I just love the city in winter. Kinda cold, but not too cold. Nice to walk around." She hesitated. "It was there. We're at that cool place on Dauphine. It's only two stories and every room has a balcony, either looking over the courtyard or the street, and every balcony has a window and a door. The *rougarou* was in the window. I saw him. And he saw me. He knows I saw him in the swamp and I think he's after me because I did."

She was close to hysterics and Quinn knew he needed to calm things down. "We can start by moving your room."

"You really think there was a *rougarou* and that it followed these young ladies to their hotel?" Larue asked, obviously trying hard not to sound so incredulous that he offended the young women.

Quinn looked at Larue, who quickly read his expression. No, he didn't think a monster had followed them. But changing rooms could appease the young women, or at the least make them feel better, as if the police were trying to do something.

His friend nodded in agreement.

"We'll get a police escort and have you out of your hotel

and into one that is right on Bourbon Street," he said. "It'll be a room over one of the hottest night spots where there are always cops and security guards. Detective Larue and I will go with you so that we can personally make an inspection. Now, bear in mind, we don't doubt what you saw. We're just not sure what you saw is really a *rougarou*." He lifted a hand as Jane was about to protest. "People in this area all know the legends about the *rougarou*. Someone out there might be using the legend. In this day and age, it's quite possible to fake a monster."

They both looked at him with huge eyes, seemingly wanting to trust in him.

"Sound like a plan?" Quinn asked Larue.

The detective nodded. "Let's move, though. We have to get out to Honey Swamp. We're going to help the task force with the investigation."

Ten minutes later they were at the hotel where the young women were staying. Quinn inspected the balcony while they gathered their belongings together. The room sat on the second floor, but the balcony might have been easily accessed from the street. There was a heavy pipe near enough for someone to crawl up and gain a grip on one of the wrought iron rails. "How did someone walk through the French Quarter all dressed up without being noticed?"

"This is New Orleans," Larue said. "Not far from Bourbon Street. Think about it, Quinn. Does anyone really notice *crazy* around here? I mean, there's a lot of crazy."

"Something like the *rougarou*? A giant man with a wolf's head?"

"Somebody walked stark naked down Bourbon Street about two days ago, and it took that long for anyone to report it to the police," Larue told him.

"That's not a *rougarou*."

Larue shrugged. "Okay. I'll give you that."

"To put a spin of logic on this, I'd say that it was more than possible for a man to dress up, then crawl up here to scare Jane and Lana. It's also possible that whoever was here had nothing to do with the murder in the swamp, or maybe someone got wind of the situation and knew that the two young women had been on the tour and decided to scare them. They're visitors, yes, but they know the city and they might have met a young man anxious to scare them. Then he comes along and offers his presence as protection against whatever has them frightened."

Larue did not argue.

"At any rate," Quinn said. "Let's go meet your friends from Pearl River."

* * * *

"I remember the murders," David said, looking into space as if he could see across the years. "My dad was so worried about my mom. He didn't want her going out at all. They found the one young woman, Genevieve LaCoste, almost where we were last night. I don't know why I remember her name so clearly. She was a mess. The medical examiner said that she'd been ripped up by animals after death. But Danni, her throat was ripped out, too. Just like the guy last night. The cops never found the killer. They insisted that there was a killer, but old Selena Duarte told them that it was the *rougarou*. She said that the young women had behaved badly. They ignored the rules of Lent and spent their nights drinking and meeting up with young men at bars."

"They never caught the killer," Danni said, "but that doesn't mean that there was a *rougarou*. Have you offended anyone, David? You or Julian? Do you know if anyone is angry with you? Someone who would do something so horrible, just to ruin your tours?"

He laughed. "There's old Selena Duarte. But she's five-foot-two and pretty fragile."

"Why is Selena upset with you?"

"She considers the swamp her personal property."

"But other companies do swamp tours there."

"Apparently, according to Selena, our night tours have awakened the spirit of the *rougarou*. We're not being respectful."

"Anyone else?" Danni asked.

She wished that Quinn was here. She wasn't sure how to help David or where to go from there. She'd learned that objects could be evil. Either within themselves or by making others believe in evil.

The *rougarou* of legend was not a thing, not inanimate. It was a beast, a creature, a monster.

"Julian is one of the nicest guys in the world. He's never offended anyone," David said. "Except for that one guy. He wanted a job with us, but Julian didn't like him. He said that he came in for the interview either stoned or drunk. And when Julian said something, the guy told him that he should be cool, 'it was like, New Orleans, and you know, we're all laid back here.' In fact, he thought that we should serve absinthe on our swamp tours, and that the captain and the guide ought to drink with everyone. You know Julian. He's a safety first kind of guy. Partying is fine on your off hours, but never when you have a responsibility. He told the guy to get out. The guy told Julian that he was going to rot in hell."

"You still have his application?" Danni asked.

"Sure. But whether people tell the truth on an application or not is another matter," David reminded her.

"Let's head over to the office. Is Julian there?"

"He should be. It's right on Chartres Street. Are we walking?"

"Yep. And we'll take Wolf with us," she told David.

Though he couldn't protect them from everything, the dog's presence might make David feel better. She hurried into the shop to tell Billie that she'd be with David and to give Quinn a heads-up if he called. Billie had Bo Ray down working with him. She left the shop with David.

As they walked down Royal Street to the corner, then to Chartres, they passed her shop window. Count D'Oro stood there, his mannequin eyes fantastically evil, his white shirt and gold vest impeccable despite the pool of fabric "blood" at his feet and the display of "*Rougarou* Repellent," voodoo-doll-like charms on the small three-pronged stool by his side. The mannequin had an evil twist to its lips and he gripped his cane with its silver wolf's head with casual ease, as if ready to move at any moment. David stopped walking and stared. It was clear that he hadn't noticed the window when he'd visited the shop in the past.

"Count D'Oro, known to have awakened the demon of the *rougarou* before his murder spree," he said.

"The man was a sick murderer long before he believed he had the power of the *rougarou*, and long before he claimed that it was the *rougarou* doing the killing," she told him.

David continued to stare at the display, then he turned to Danni. "He claimed that the *rougarou* did the killing. Others claimed that he turned into the *rougarou*, that his head became the head of a vicious wolf-like monster with mammoth, ripping teeth. Supposedly, he used that cane to bash heads in."

"That cane is plastic, David. It's just a display."

"Of course," he murmured, laying his hand on Wolf's head. "Let's go talk to Julian about the weird guy who applied for a job. But from what he said, the guy wasn't much of a *rougarou*. More like an idiot."

He started walking.

She followed him, glancing back at her own display.

Strange.

It seemed like the smile on the mannequin of Count D'Oro had widened.

Ever so slightly.

* * * *

The two cops from Pearl River seemed like solid guys. Hayden Beauchamp was young, fairly new to the force, slim, fit, and a bit in awe of the older Dirk Deerfield.

Deerfield was a twenty-five-year vet with the force. Larue had told Quinn that he was planning his retirement in another five years. Before being with the Pearl River force, he'd spent five years with the LAPD. He was weathered, easy, and confident, and he'd heard about Quinn.

In fact, he'd seen him play football.

"There was a professional career out there for you," he told Quinn after shaking his hand. "Can't say as that I'd not have chosen football over police work or investigation."

Quinn shook his head. "Football honestly wasn't that kind to me. I think I'm where I'm supposed to be now."

They'd met at the station and gone through the medical examiner's initial notes. Then they looked at the crime scene photos.

"Thing is, the bayou isn't kind," Deerfield said. "We had police and forensic crews out to the site within the hour. But all the blood and other matter had dispersed. A few creatures were already nibbling on the corpse. We're lucky a hungry gator didn't just take it down."

"Shall we see the site?" Larue asked.

Deerfield nodded. "You can, but there's nothing to find. Crews went over the area. Not a single piece of evidence. Not even litter thrown out by a passersby. But, sure, we can head to the site. All this harkens back to some bad stuff about twenty years ago."

"I remember," Quinn said.

"I even remember," Beauchamp added. "I was just a kid back then, but I remember. I can't believe that I'm working with a cop who was on that case. Sad and amazing. All that, and the killer got away."

"Still haunts me," Deerfield said. "We never caught that guy. From what I understand, though, it wouldn't make much sense for this to be the same perpetrator. From the classes they send us to, I understand that such a killer either gets worse, gets caught, or gets dead. He just doesn't stop for twenty years. And that *rougarou* bull that goes around? What? Some wolf-headed, old Cajun legend hides out for twenty years without anyone catching sight of it? I don't think so."

"You're thinking some kind of a copycat killer?" Larue asked Deerfield.

"Could be. Regardless, he needs to be caught. Three young women. Lovely, sweet girls. And we had nothing. Boyfriend of one was seen by dozens of people working. We checked out the local tours, the neighbors, you name it. We had no forensic evidence. It was a nightmare."

"Just like here," Quinn asked. "The same. Down to the details?"

"Same method of murder," Deerfield said wearily. "But this time the victim was a man. Someone has been studying the past."

"Autopsy was first thing this morning," Beauchamp said. "Rush on everything, and since so much of his skull was cracked in, throat all ripped up, and him in the water, the ID became a challenge. We can't just put a picture of him out in the papers. No fingerprints matched anything we have, but we do have some dental charts in our missing persons report."

"Bring up the autopsy report, will you, Hayden?" Deerfield asked Beauchamp.

Quinn lowered his head to hide a small smile. Deerfield was key in that partnership. Older, more experienced, aware of the pitfalls. Beauchamp pulled his weight in their partnership with tech expertise, his phone the size of a notepad, and he had the report up as Deerfield finished speaking.

"White male between the age of twenty-eight and thirty-four. Five-feet-ten-inches tall. One-hundred and seventy-five pounds. Last meal—crawfish etouffee, grits, and asparagus. He'd eaten somewhere in the hour and a half before his death, and Doc Melloni has been around a while. He knew right away, which is good. Thing is, most places out here do serve crawfish etouffee."

"We're still checking out local restaurants and cafes, and at least they're a little sparser out in this area than they are in the city. Of course, he could have been in the city and made it out here just in time to have his head bashed in and throat ripped out." Deerfield shook his head. "Anyway, as you can see, the man was in excellent health, fit and sound before his demise."

"He might have lived to a hundred," Beauchamp said sadly.

Twenty minutes later, the four of them headed out with a young officer in a police boat, straight to the spot where the body had been found.

Deerfield did the talking, pointing to the shore.

"Body was there, right at the edge of the water, mostly head first, or what was left of the head. Feet were caught up on the high grasses. As you can see, the trees are pretty heavy around here. You've got a fair distance to the road. Course, you've got a few businesses dotting the shoreline, not too close. And you're a football field from here out to the highway. Locals come around, as do the tour boats. But it's pretty isolated. That's what's hard to figure. What was a guy in a business suit and Gucci loafers doing out in this part of the swamp?"

"We're expecting to get an ID on him soon," Beauchamp said. "No wallet on him, but pretty damned weird for a robbery. I mean, it was overkill."

"Can you get me in a little closer?" Quinn asked the captain.

The man nodded and eased the boat toward the muddy shoreline.

Quinn jumped out.

The grasses and mud were heavy right where the corpse had been found. Thick trees sprouted from the more solid ground further in. As Deerfield had pointed out, they weren't that far from the highway. He could hear the traffic in the distance.

"The victim was killed right here, right on the shoreline. The blow to the back of his head was first?" Quinn asked.

"That's what the medical examiner concluded," Deerfield said. "The victim had to have been standing near the water. He was then twisted around for the attack on the throat."

"And human teeth could have done the damage?" Quinn asked skeptically.

Deerfield shrugged. "Enhanced human teeth, maybe? People do all kinds of crazy things. We got one of those whacky vampire cults out here, you know. Heaven help us. They use pig's blood in their rituals, keeping it legal and all, but I've seen some of them with their teeth all filed to points. But was there some other kind of creature involved? We don't know, as yet. And I'm not so sure testing will get us the answers."

"Okay, so the killer could have parked up on the road. Possibly came in from the city. I know I go into the French Quarter often. Easy enough," Beauchamp said.

"Ah, easy when you're young and good-looking," Deerfield said lightly. "But, sure, simple enough to get into the city and out."

"Maybe he went into the city and lured the guy out here

somehow," Beauchamp said. "The victim trusted him, thinking they were coming out here for something else."

"It's possible," Deerfield said, smiling at his young protégé.

"Could have arrived via some kind of boat?" Quinn asked. "Anyone on the tour report seeing any other boats in the area?"

"No," Deerfield said, "but, yeah, they could have come by boat. Thing is, we haven't found any unknown cars parked in the area."

"The car could be down in Honey Swamp somewhere," Quinn said, pointing to the road. "Easy enough for someone to escape that way. The young women this morning reported that something was moving through the trees. The killer, I'd say. So he went back to the road, jumped in a car, and drove away."

"Unless it was a *rougarou*," Beauchamp suggested, shrugging. "In which case, it's still hiding out there in the woods. Waiting."

Or it ran back to New Orleans to watch young women in their hotel rooms, Quinn thought.

"I have to apologize," Deerfield said. "Hayden has really studied the old case."

"It's kind of like Jack the Ripper. You can't help coming up with theories. And a lot of the locals do believe in the *rougarou*," Beauchamp said.

Deerfield shook his head. "I don't believe in the *rougarou* or in witches, good or bad. I do believe that there was a killer before who was clever. And now we have a new one. Anyway, we're glad for your help. We don't want to fail again. Ready to head back in?"

Quinn nodded and climbed back in the boat.

They drifted away from the shoreline and the engine roared to life.

"Stop," Quinn shouted.

"What?" Larue demanded, startled. "Quinn—"

"You see something?" Deerfield asked, perplexed. "We

looked all over last night and into the morning. They didn't find—"

"Over there. Bring the boat closer to shore again." Quinn pointed. "There."

The others stared for a moment and he understood why. He wasn't sure how he'd seen the body floating himself. The victim's hair was as dark as the water beneath the shade of the trees, her clothing a mottled green.

"Oh, no," Beauchamp breathed.

"Another victim," Larue said, reaching over the hull of the police cruiser and turning the body.

The left portion of her head and face were obliterated, her throat slashed to the bone.

"Oh, my God," Beauchamp whispered.

* * * *

Danni and David reached the tour company's booking office on Chartres Street. David introduced their reservationist, a grave young woman with beautiful golden mahogany skin, big hazel eyes, and dark hair. Her name was Sandy Richardson. She attempted a smile for Danni.

"I can guarantee you that whatever tour you take with us, you'll be informed and entertained. We're truly one of the best companies you'll ever find."

"Danni is an old friend, Sandy," David said.

"Oh," Sandy said. "In that case, I should tell you that people are furious. They don't want you canceling the bayou night tour. One guy told me that he'd be out there with his shotgun, and no *rougarou* or swamp thing or any other creature would get his hands on anyone."

"Unfortunately, this kind of thing draws all the weekend warriors out," David said wearily. "Did you say that we were closing the tour only temporarily?"

"I did. Your weekend warrior wants to head out with a boat anyway," Sandy said.

"Best of luck to him," David murmured. "Is Julian back in the office?"

She followed David down a narrow hallway to a half open door. Julian Henri, a slim young man with a shock of dark hair and serious eyes, was seated at a desk, shoulders slumped as he stared at his computer.

He looked up as they entered the room, his eyes flickering with recognition. "Danni Cafferty? You look great. How are you?"

She smiled. "Good. Thanks, Julian. Glad to see you. Sorry about the circumstances."

"Yeah, thanks." Then he frowned, looking at David. "Oh, no. You went to Danni's because of the rumors when we were young? That her father collected things that were haunted or evil. Danni, I'm so sorry."

"No problem, Julian, really," she said. "I'm not sure what we can do, but—"

"Yeah, that's right. I've heard. You're with Michael Quinn."

"You know Quinn?" Danni asked.

"I know of him," Julian said. "And it sounds good. I'm happy for you both. This thing with the tour is horrible and scary. There could be more. And you can't believe the e-mails we're getting. I'll read you one of my favorites." He tapped the keyboard on his desk. "'You irresponsible asses. A few years up north and you forget who you are and what you came from. Money hungry asses. You've awakened the *rougarou*. Death is on your hands. You're murderers.' Here's another one, really concise. 'Fuck you, monster men.'" He shook his head and looked up. "Do you believe this crap?"

"Why not?" David asked wearily. "There are television

shows dedicated to chasing the yeti or abominable snowman. People love legends more than the truth."

"And," Danni said, "some people are just superstitious, and really stupid, cruel, rude, and horrible. It'll go away when the police find the killer."

Julian looked up at her. He was about her age, still not thirty, but looked younger with thin dark hair and wide eyes. Usually quick to smile, today he looked as if he was simply beaten down.

"They didn't catch the guy when we were kids," he said. "Could that same murderer have waited for twenty years to start over again? Or did we somehow really awaken the soul of Count D'Oro and let him run around as a *rougarou* again?"

"Someone is obviously playing on legend," Danni said. "Julian, did you see anything?"

He shook his head with disgust. "I was just maneuvering through the swamp, like I've done most of my life. We had a good group on board. They listened, joked around, laughing. It was good. Then I heard the scream and saw the body."

"What about the young man you didn't hire? David said that you don't have any enemies, but that you didn't hire a guy who was being a jerk."

"That guy? He didn't seem smart enough to kill anyone. Maybe you don't have to be smart. His name was—" He paused and hit a few keys on his computer again. "Jim Novak. Thirty-three. No college. But somehow graduated high school. He claimed that he'd been a tour guide in Savannah. I never tried to verify his résumé since I knew we weren't hiring him."

"Address?" Danni asked.

Julian drew a notepad toward him, checked the computer screen, and scribbled down the address. He handed the paper to her.

"Can you think of anyone else who might not want you

guys to make a success of this tour? Or anyone who might want to somehow use the two of you as scapegoats?"

Julian looked at David. "What's her face? The woman who owns that other tour company. Victoria—"

"Miller," David added.

"She was ticked-off about us doing this tour," Julian said.

"I think she was madder because her boyfriend, that Gene Andre guy, thought it was a great idea. And then there's the realtor, your dad's old friend, Julian," David said.

"He wanted to buy the property with the docks," Julian said. "Guess they're pretty worthless now."

"What's the guy's name?" she asked. "There are lots of realtors around."

"Byron Grayson. Old, smart-looking dude," Julian said. "Always in a gray suit."

"To be honest," David said. "I can't even imagine him in the swamp."

Danni nodded. "I'm going to head back and start doing some research. Here's the thing, whoever killed that man knew the legends. I'll see what I can find."

"I'll walk back with you," David said. "Julian, I'll be back—"

"I'm going home to my apartment, not out to any of the shacks by Honey Swamp," Julian said. "I'm going to duck and cover for a while."

"We will figure this out," Danni said,

But what if they couldn't? They were talking about the swamp.

A great place to hide a million sins.

She said good-bye to Julian and Sandy, then she and David walked the few blocks from the Legends office back to the Cheshire Cat. They came through the shop and spoke briefly with Billie and Bo Ray. They'd both seen the news and knew what was going on.

Back in the kitchen with David, she drew out her laptop and began searching for all the information she could find about the *rougarou*, Honey Swamp, and the murders that had taken place there.

"Julian's family owns that property," David said. "They've owned it since before the Civil War. If I understand it, they bought it from the parish after Count D'Oro met with vigilante justice. That's why Julian is afraid people will blame this on him."

"David, the legend of the *rougarou* was around long before Count D'Oro," Danni reminded him. "Julian can't really believe that this is his fault in any way."

"But he does."

"He blames himself because you two are doing tours? Come on. Many companies do bayou tours."

She heard a key twist in the courtyard door that led straight into the kitchen and looked up to see Quinn enter. He walked in looking weary, his dark hair tousled, eyes grave. And he immediately noted David in the chair.

Quinn had grown up in the Garden District. He was older than Danni and David by several years. He glanced at David, then at Danni, and she realized that they'd never met.

"Quinn, this is David Fagin," she said, rising.

David rose to shake hands. "So you're the 'Mighty Quinn.'"

"I am Quinn. Not sure about mighty." He visibly relaxed with the handshake. "Does you being here have anything to do with the bodies in the bayou?"

"Yes. Wait. Bodies? I only knew about the one," David said.

"Count is up to two," Quinn replied. "We found a second victim, a young woman, this afternoon."

He was quiet a minute and then looked over at Danni.

"Actually, *I* found her."

Chapter 3

The basement wasn't really a basement. The rest of the house was built up, allowing for a basement in an area that could flood. The first French fur trappers had chosen wisely when they had settled in the French Quarter. It was the highest ground around. Which wasn't saying much since most of New Orleans was below sea level. The Cheshire Cat's basement had been Danni's father's office, the place where he'd housed his private collection and *The Book of Truth*. Quinn knew that Danni had not known of the existence of the book until the day her father died. Angus had talked about the book, but Quinn himself hadn't seen it until he and Danni had been forced to seek its guidance.

Called *The Book of Truth*, it might have been better labeled *The Book of Fantasy and Legend*. It noted creatures from every culture and society, from vampires and werewolves to "fairy folk" and beyond. When, exactly, it had been written they didn't know. It appeared to be medieval, coming from a time when the world was filled with superstition and feared darkness and the devil. But the book was also filled with curious bits of history that often helped. Like how to kill vampire, which they'd not as yet studied, though they had made use of other parts in curious ways.

Quinn perched on Angus's desk, glancing at the various objects that were piled here and there. Some Greek, Egyptian, medieval, and Victorian era pieces. Crates and boxes littered the room, some labeled DO NOT OPEN.

Danni sat reading.

David had gone, headed to his own apartment in the city to hide out. Danni had told Quinn everything David and Julian had said. Many people in New Orleans were transient, most had come to the city, fallen in love with it, and stayed. Others had been there forever and would never leave. It was possible that all the hate e-mails were just superstitious locals.

"'*Rougarou*,'" Danni read from one of the books. "'French, cultural, regional, similar to other creatures born of evil, caught in the web of sin, sometimes, the sins of others. Eater of men's souls. Silver does not slayeth this beast, only the cleansing of fire will lay it to rest.'"

"That's it?" Quinn asked.

"That I can find," she said. "Quinn, what about the murders twenty years ago? You probably remember more than I do."

"I remember that my parents wouldn't let me anywhere near Honey Swamp. It was only young women who were killed, but it was as if a monster suddenly arose out of the earth. They never found a single clue as to who had murdered those women. The thing is, when you find a body in a swamp, even now, it's hard to find any kind of evidence."

He paused, thinking.

"David said that his name was written in the mud and the police didn't see it. What if David imagined what was written? Maybe this has nothing to do with them. Then again, maybe it does. I say we check out the guy who applied for the job. Then, the realtor and the tour group lady."

"Jim Novak, Byron Grayson, and Victoria Miller. They mentioned her boyfriend or partner, too, a guy named Gene

Andre. Andre apparently approved of their tour, which pissed off Victoria Miller. Quinn," she asked, blue eyes wide and somber, "shouldn't we be looking into the past? Or calling on Natasha, maybe."

"You want to suggest this has to do with voodoo?"

"Certainly not. But Natasha has connections on the street, and she'll remember the past better than we do." She winced, looking at him sadly. "We could definitely get together with her and Father Ryan. At the very least, they're older and both have excellent memories."

Quinn nodded. Father Ryan was a most unusual priest. Excellent at what was expected of him in his calling, capable of much more. He'd been there with Quinn's parents when he'd flatlined. He'd been there when stranger things had happened and hadn't even blinked. Maybe his faith allowed him to see beyond what others were willing to accept.

Natasha Laroche—Mistress LaBelle—owned a voodoo shop just down the street. She was one of the most regal women Quinn had ever known. She sold the usual, gris-gris, statues, herbs, and all the customary voodoo paraphernalia, and read tealeaves, palms, tarot cards and more. But she was also a priestess with a devout following. She and Father Ryan, despite their passions to their own religions, seemed to have everything in common and worked exceptionally well together. Part of an odd assembly of strange crime fighters, and also great friends.

"You go and see Natasha," Quinn said. "I'll check out this address and pick up Father Ryan."

He stood. Wolf, who had been sleeping at his feet, hopped up too.

"You stay and watch over Danni," Quinn told the dog.

"I could swear he heard you mention Father Ryan," Danni said. "Take Wolf with you. I'm fine. I'm nowhere near Honey Swamp and Natasha is just down the street. They should both be ready for whatever. We had intended to go out tonight, remember?"

Quinn nodded and paused to kiss the top of her head. For a moment, he didn't want to leave her, not even for a second. Her hair always smelled so clean and yet so evocative. He wanted to forget all about *rougarous* and dead bodies in the swamp. He even wanted to forget about a night out with music and friends. Lock the world away. Play out a scene from *Gone with the Wind* and sweep Danni off her feet, carry her up the stairs, dive into the comfort of their bed and the sensuality of her bare flesh.

"Quinn?"

He snapped back to reality. "Yeah, I'm going."

He headed for the door.

The phone rang.

It was Jake Larue.

"I'm sure as hell not saying that there was a *rougarou* out there last night," he told Quinn.

He heard the "but" in Larue's voice.

"But the guy did follow those young women back to the city. The blood on their balcony matched that of the first victim. The man found last night in the bayou."

* * * *

Jez, Natasha's unbelievably handsome, mixed-race assistant, had apparently been told that Danni was coming. Natasha always seemed to know these things, exuding an air of mystery in her manner and demeanor. Jez informed her that Natasha was waiting in the courtyard.

Natasha was wearing a colorful dress and a turban to match, all in shades of orange and gold that enhanced the dusky quality of her skin. She sat at one of her wrought iron tables, a pile of books at her side. She rose and enveloped Danni in a hug, and then indicated they should both sit.

"No music tonight?" Natasha asked.

Danni shook her head. "Tell me what you know?"

"Quite a bit, actually. I went and looked up the old murders as soon as I heard what happened."

"The young women killed twenty years ago?" Danni asked.

"No, I went way further back, all the way to Melissa DeVane."

"I don't remember the name. Was she one of the victims?"

"She was, but not twenty years ago. When the French lost this area to the Spanish, Spain didn't even send a governor right away. The French more or less refused to acknowledge what was going on. I know you've heard of Count D'Oro."

"He wanted the Good Witch of Honey Swamp—"

"Melissa DeVane."

She connected the dots.

"Count Otto D'Oro was a horrible man. Richer than can be imagined. He had many mistresses, and many of them disappeared. Nothing could be proven against the man. He was very powerful. It was said that he had his own army of enforcers. He was into everything. Prostitution, gambling, piracy, you name it. But Melissa lived out in Honey Swamp. She was reputed to be able to cure the sick, to make crops grow, even to bring the rain. She never did anything evil. And she was beautiful. Naturally, D'Oro wanted her."

"And she didn't want a thing to do with him." Danni could tell where the story was going.

"But he kept insisting. The story goes that she caused rain and a flood, leaving him trapped with some of his minions in the swamp. He was furious, so he waited for the floodwaters to recede, then sent his minions to get her. He tied her to a tree and threatened to burn her alive. She said that she'd rather kiss flames than him. Supposed eyewitness accounts claim that the rains came again when he tried to burn her. In the end, though, it couldn't rain enough to dampen his enthusiasm. Eventually, he got a fire going. And that was when she cursed him. People say that he then turned into the *rougarou*—because his soul had been consumed by evil. And, as you've heard, he was eventually hunted down. Even his own people turned on him. And, he, too, was finally burned alive and the murders in Honey Swamp came to an end. Here's the thing. He carried a cane with a silver wolf's head. Like the cane of the mannequin in your window."

"I need to get that display down," Danni said. "What about the cane?"

"Apparently, D'Oro had some kind of an evil magician, or warlock, or whatever one chooses to call such a man in his employ, nowhere near as gifted as the white witch and certainly nowhere near as beautiful. The silver wolf's head on the cane absorbed the brunt of the curse, and that's what made D'Oro become a *rougarou* rather than falling victim to one himself."

"You think that the cane causes the evil?" Danni asked. "But it's not in any museum that I've ever heard about. And D'Oro wasn't buried. His ashes were left to disperse into Honey Swamp, along with whatever was left of his bones."

"That would make one assume that, somewhere in Honey Swamp are the remnants of that cane," Natasha said. "Unless, of course, someone found it."

"That's a long shot," Danni said.

Natasha was thoughtful. "It brings us back to the question of what evil *is*. Greed, lust? Hatred?"

"The world and the human mind are complex, Natasha. People kill for a lot of reasons. They torture and commit atrocities for their own goals and agendas. And then again, is someone with a totally fractured mind evil or just broken?"

"I don't know about every circumstance," Natasha said. "But what's going on here is evil, by any definition." She paused.

"The mind is powerful. We all know that. If you believe that you have an incredible power granted to you by the devil, or simple evil, can you make it so? Perception can be a form of truth."

"You're right about that," Danni murmured. "So what do we do? Search the swamp. Search the streets for someone with a silver wolf's head cane? Or look to the reasons people become evil? Natasha, two young women were on the tour boat that came upon the first victim. The one young lady was convinced that she saw a *rougarou* on her hotel balcony."

"We can believe we see many things," Natasha said.

"But there was blood on the balcony that matched the blood of the first victim. Detective Jake Larue just called Quinn. Whoever killed that first victim came into the French Quarter as a *rougarou*."

Natasha sat in silence for a minute. Then she lifted one of the books from the stack at her side.

"This is on the murders from twenty years ago. There was one young lady named Genevieve LaCoste. She was a shopkeeper in the Garden District. She'd been out with a boyfriend to Honey Swamp the day she was killed. She'd come back to the city, but was found the next day, dead, in the swamp. Maybe, just maybe, this *rougarou* sees what he wants and comes after it. Your young lady was very lucky to escape him."

"She wasn't alone. She was with a friend."

"Maybe the *rougarou* expected her to be alone. Or maybe whoever was pretending to be a *rougarou* was startled away by her screams or something from the street," Natasha suggested. "Read more of the book. Twenty years ago wasn't the first time people were found ripped apart in the swamp. It happened eighty years and about a hundred and fifty years ago, too. There was nothing about it with rhyme or reason, just every twenty or fifty years, that kind of thing. But it happened first with Count D'Oro, and it's happened again and again through the years."

"No rhyme or reason," Danni mused. "Except that, there has to be a reason. We just don't know what it is yet."

"Evil."

"And evil is usually personified. There's an evil man out there. We have to find out who he is." Danni rose. "I think I'm going to check on the value of my property."

"What?" Natasha asked.

"Pay a visit to a realtor," Danni said. "Meet me back at my place in about two hours?"

"I'll be there."

* * * *

Father John Ryan lived in the rectory by the church.

He stood to almost Quinn's height, leanly muscled, bald, and equipped with sharp gray eyes that seemed to quickly assess people and problems. Born in Ireland, he'd served in the heart of Africa and various other places where he'd acquired knowledge about many cultures, peoples, and religions. Not a man to judge, instead more one to evaluate and appreciate.

"I was expecting you," the priest told Quinn. "And Wolf, of course." Father Ryan greeted the mammoth dog with affection. "I assumed there would be no music tonight. So what do you know so far? I'm assuming you're here because of the murders in the swamps? They just announced that a second body was found."

Quinn nodded.

But before he could speak, Father Ryan said, "Now I get it. You found the second victim."

He nodded. "What do you know about the Wolfman murders twenty years ago? Were you here then?"

"I'd just arrived in New Orleans," Ryan said. "And yes, I do remember. It was all horrible. One of the young women killed was local. I presided at her funeral."

"Tell me about her."

"Genevieve. I'd met her only briefly. She was such a beautiful young lady. Striking in every way. She ran a shop in the Garden District and grew up here. She went all the way through Loyola, a stellar student in the business school. Her shop was wonderful and she was eager to take more classes. To do good things. Her death was tragic, and the police were determined. But it was one of those cases where the swamp consumed all the evidence. After her death, the murders stopped."

"But there were other victims," Quinn said.

"Both lovely young women." Father Ryan paused, deep in memory. "Patricia Ahern and Sonia Gavin. The one was from New York City. The other a Texan, I think. They'd been in New Orleans on vacation. I know the police investigated all the tour operators at the time since both girls had been on tours. Of course, Genevieve hadn't been on a tour, but she'd been out in the swamp with her boyfriend the day before. He was a suspect, but was cleared. He'd been back at work in his father's bar all through the night."

"I heard a little on the past this morning. Detective Deerfield was working back then, too. Those murders fell to the Pearl River department. Those guys seem to think that someone definitely knows about the past murders and all the local lore. Which, I suppose, would point to a local. Only this time we have a male victim. Years ago they were all beautiful young women. I keep thinking, why? What was happening then, and can it have anything to do with what's happening now? Seldom does a savage killer wait around twenty years to start all over again."

"Unless he was in prison," Ryan said. "But the cops are good. Larue and the Pearl River men will be checking for anyone who might have gotten back out. I still think that we'd have heard about a killer brought in who'd done anything like this.

There's a connection with the past murders. There's probably a connection back to the D'Oro and the Good Witch and the *rougarou* story. One murder last night, another today. This killer is on a spree. We have to move on this."

"What do you suggest?"

"Meeting at the house tonight. But we may have something."

Quinn went on to tell Father Ryan about David Fagin and Julian Henri, their new swamp tour, and the e-mails they received.

"Rival tour group?" Father Ryan said doubtfully. "That's pretty drastic, brutally murdering people as a means of getting rid of competition."

Quinn's phone buzzed.

He checked the display.

Danni had sent him a text.

Back at the Cheshire Cat at 7:00?

He hit the *O* and *K* keys and sent his message, then looked at Father Ryan. "Want to check out the local competition?"

"Sounds like a plan. That is, of course, as long as we're sending someone out for dinner once we get there."

Quinn pulled out his phone again. Victoria Miller owned Crescent City Sites. The reservation office was on Decatur Street, about a block from Jackson Square.

"We taking Wolf with us?" Father Ryan asked.

"Hell, yeah," Quinn said. "Wolf is always up for a good swamp tour, aren't you, boy?"

The dog barked his agreement.

They headed out to Quinn's car. It wasn't much of a drive, but the evening had turned cold. The streets of the French Quarter were heavy with pedestrian traffic and finding a place to park on the riverfront took some time. From there it took them only a matter of minutes to reach the tour offices. The doors were closed against the cold. Quinn pushed them open. Wolf followed first, then Father Ryan. The woman behind the counter was probably in her early forties, the kind though who would be a beauty at any stage of life. Her features were delicate, her body slim. She was dressed in a tight red sweater that enhanced the platinum color of her hair and the brilliant shade of her green eyes. She smiled at first in welcome, then seemed to shrink back as she noted Wolf.

"Sorry," Quinn said quickly. "I'll have him wait outside."

"No, it's all right. He just startled me. Your dog is the size of a pony. Come in, please. What are you looking for? Actually, I should tell you we really can't allow the dog on the swamp or plantation tours. Though honestly, for a walking tour, if you wanted to hang in the back, I suppose it would be okay. I'm getting ahead of myself. What kind of a tour are you looking to take? I'm Victoria Miller."

"Michael Quinn, and this is my dog, Wolf. And the tall gentleman behind me is Father John Ryan."

"Nice to meet you," she said, frowning. "You're an unlikely tour group."

"Honestly, we're here because of the murders in Honey Swamp," Quinn said.

"Oh." Her fine features grew taut. "We don't do murder site tours."

"I'm a private investigator, working with the police," Quinn said.

She shook her head, as if baffled. "Why are you here? Legends is the company that was involved. It was one of the Legends boats that came upon the body of that poor man."

"Yes, but you have boats out there all the time, don't you?" Quinn asked.

"We don't do anything like a ridiculous monster tour." The tone of her voice indicated that it was offensive that anyone might even think such a thing.

Quinn picked up one of the brochures advertising a vampire tour. "But these are okay?"

"That's different. We do vampire tours that include facts about Anne Rice, the craze that went around because of her books, the people in the city who practice 'spiritual' vampirism, and the cults who drink animal blood. We try hard to keep facts and history in our tours."

"Sounds enterprising," Quinn said, offering her his best smile. "We were hoping you might have some clue as to what's going on in the swamp. If there have been strangers hanging out around any of the docks. If you've seen anything unusual. You do own a big tour group, known for blending fact with fun."

That mollified her ego.

"I have to admit," she said. "I thought it was ridiculous that David and Julian wanted to start their own thing. I wanted to buy Julian's property. It could have helped us. I mean, he was already running tours in the city and out to the plantations. There are a zillion tour groups working around here. We didn't need another one. And as far as the swamp goes, I'd check it all out with some of the realtors who keep trying to buy property."

"Are you from this area?"

She tossed back her long blond mane. "I'm from New England. But don't go thinking that doesn't make me every bit as good as the Legends guys. Those of us who aren't from here love the area with a greater passion. We research whatever everyone else thinks that they know. We're good. No. We're excellent. But the two little college brats wanted to usurp my business."

"Did you threaten them?" He smiled as he added, "Or send them a few e-mails?"

"I wouldn't stoop so low," Victoria said. "Now, you gentlemen are not the police. And if you were, I couldn't help you anyway. If you don't mind, I'm busy."

He glanced around at the empty office. "I can see that you are."

He, Father Ryan, and Wolf headed for the door. But before they left, the priest nudged him. A door was ajar to a back office. Inside, a young man sat, watching, listening. He saw that Quinn and Father Ryan had spotted him. He nodded, as if he was aware they needed answers that could not be provided then.

Quinn lowered his head in acknowledgement.

Message received.

And they left.

* * * *

A receptionist told Danni that Byron Grayson would be right with her, but after twenty minutes she still sat in the waiting room. His offices were down in the Central Business District, near the convention center. He must have been doing well enough as the offices were elegant. Plush sofas and a wide screen television adorned the waiting room, along with a pod coffee maker. A visitor could also grab a power bar or read any one of a number of high-end magazines.

She rose and approached the receptionist's desk. "Excuse me. Is Mr. Grayson available this evening? If not, perhaps—"

"I sent him a message ages ago that you were here," the receptionist said. "Let me buzz through to his office. He's usually out as soon as I let him know we have a new client."

Another buzz, but no answer.

"I thought he was back there," the receptionist said. "I had a list of items that needed to be attended to on my desk this morning."

"You mean you haven't seen him all day?" Danni asked.

"I don't disturb Mr. Grayson," she said. "If you'll just wait a minute, I'll see what's keeping him."

The receptionist started down a hallway. Danni held back, and then followed behind her. A knock on a closed door went unanswered so the woman opened it.

And screamed.

Danni ran up behind her and looked in, expecting to see a dead man.

But there was no one there.

Only a massive pool of blood spilled over Grayson's desk, dripping onto the rich beige carpet in little crimson waves.

Chapter 4

Quinn and Larue arrived at the offices of Byron Grayson at about the same time. Larue was accompanied by sirens blazing and Quinn with Father Ryan and Wolf. He left the priest and the dog on the street and hurried into the realtor's office. Danni sat in the waiting area, her arms around the shoulders of a young woman, shaking with fear. Larue was hunkering down to talk to her as the forensic people worked in Grayson's office.

"All day, I was sitting there. All day," the woman said. "And something like this was happening." She turned wide eyes to ask a question, but not to Larue. Instead, to Danni. "Oh, my God, the *rougarou*. It's real and came into the city. It rushed by me when I wasn't looking and ate poor Mr. Grayson while I was sitting right out at the reception area."

"There's a lot of blood in there," Danni told the girl. "But that doesn't mean that a *rougarou* went by you—"

"Oh, but it had to have gone by me. Oh, my God, it could have eaten me. Do you think that it came in through a window? Can a *rougarou* crawl on walls? Maybe it was in here all night? But it had to have waited to eat him. He left instructions on my desk. You see, I never bother him. What he needs he tells me, and I announce clients, and they come out. Don't think he's a mean man. He isn't mean at all. He's a great boss. He just works best that way. Says he's like a really old computer, though he still doesn't understand computers completely. And he only likes to have one window open at a time. He has to be dead. Mr. Grayson. Eaten. Oh, oh, how horrible."

She began to sob.

Quinn walked over to the waiting room sofa and hunkered down by Larue. "Miss—"

"Jensen, Belinda Jensen," the woman murmured.

"When did you last see your boss?" Quinn asked.

"Last night, closing time. But I know he was here this morning. He left paperwork for some closings on my desk."

"But you didn't see him all day?" Larue asked.

Belinda shook her head. "But that's not unusual. Mr. Grayson stays in his office, sometimes without me seeing him. I just announce things to him through the intercom. He comes out as soon as he can when we have clients. Every once in a while he comes out and says let's go to lunch. He's a good boss. But when he's working, he's working."

One of the forensic techs stepped back into the waiting room and grabbed Larue's attention. The detective stepped over to the young man. Quinn rose too and walked toward the tech and Larue.

"It's all right. Mr. Quinn is working this with us," Larue said to the tech. "What is it?"

They were all thinking that Byron Grayson, a realtor, frequently in a suit, might be their first victim. But Grayson couldn't be the body they'd found in the swamp. Grayson was an older man. Their corpse had been that of a man in his thirties. So neither victim had yet to be identified.

"It's not human blood," the tech said. "We're not sure what it is, but it's not human blood."

"Not sure what it is? Paint or something like that?" Larue

asked.

"No, it's blood, all right. Just not human."

"Animal?"

"Has to be. We're just not sure what kind of animal."

* * * *

"I'll see that Natasha gets down the block," Billie told Quinn, standing.

They'd finally all met at Danni's house on Royal Street. Father Ryan, Natasha, Danni, and Quinn, along with Bo Ray and Billie McDougal. Everything they all knew had been exchanged. Danni would keep researching the past murders and more about Byron Grayson's business. Bo Ray and Billie would hold down the shop and keep their eyes and ears open. Father Ryan and Quinn were going to head back to Honey Swamp and speak to the owners of the shacks and homes around the area. First up, of course, would be Julian Henri's old place. Easy enough—they had Julian's permission to tear it apart, top to bottom.

"Maybe there are some secret places where the *rougarou* has been hiding all these years," Bo Ray said.

"I don't think that there is a *rougarou*," Danni said.

They all looked at her.

"You know we've all discovered that strange things happen in this world," Father Ryan said.

"They find new critters all the time, animals we thought were extinct," Billie pointed out. "Maybe such beasts have existed for years. Maybe there is something like an abominable snowman or the Loch Ness monster."

"We do tend to believe in only what we see," Father Ryan said. "And since my life is based on a belief in what I don't see, I never deny the possibilities."

"I think there's something more than a creature that just

pops up at certain times," Danni said. "I mean, we don't know what went on years and years ago, and people have disappeared in swamps and never been seen again many times." She stood and gathered up a few of the paper plates they'd used for the pizza they'd ordered for dinner. "This time, I think there is a more logical answer. There's something that we just haven't discovered yet."

"The two young ladies on the boat said that a *rougarou* was outside their window," Natasha said. "They found blood on the balcony, the blood of the first victim. And now, there's a man who is missing with an unidentifiable blood left all over his office."

"I know," Danni said. "And I don't dispute the fact that there might be some kind of living creature that science hasn't discovered, captured, or realized yet. I just still keep thinking back to Count D'Oro."

"And a curse?" Father Ryan asked.

"I'm not thinking curse so much as bad human behavior," Danni said. "Count D'Oro was a horrid person, a sick killer. He wanted Melissa DeVane. By historic accounts, she was young, beautiful, filled with vitality."

"I get it," Bo Ray said. "She thought he was like dung on a shoe, and that made him want to have her all the more. And she turned him down."

"Did she make it rain? Or did it rain because it was Southern Louisiana?" Danni nodded. "The thing is, yes, all the *rougarou* killing came about. But the count wanted something."

Billie frowned. "One of the victims killed is male. Another female. And, unless I don't know everything, there was no sexual assault."

"Not everyone is after sex," Danni said.

"Most people," Bo Ray assured her. "I mean, you two, you and Quinn, you're at it—sorry, sorry. Together all the time, so you don't realize—"

"Bo Ray," Quinn said.

"Sorry, sorry."

"He's a Texan." Father Ryan lowered his head to hide a small smile. "Texans can't help themselves. They just say it like it is."

Danni wagged a plastic fork at them all. "David believes that he was personally threatened with the writing in the mud. Someone wants something. Julian Henri owns some great property, if you're into swamp tours and history. I think we're all supposed to believe what's happening is a throwback, and that it all has to do with a *rougarou*. But I don't buy it."

"Okay, in the morning everyone is on it," Quinn said. "Let's all get some sleep.

"I'll see to Natasha," Father Ryan said. "You all just hunker in for the night."

Danni went to walk Father Ryan and Natasha out through the front of the shop and lock up. Bo Ray and Billie finished cleaning up and headed for the stairs to the third floor attic where they had their apartments. Quinn put through a call to Larue. With what they'd heard about the previous murders, he wanted to make sure that the two young women who'd received the balcony visit were safe. Larue assured him that he had a man on guard at the new hotel where they'd been taken.

"Inside room," Larue told him. "No balcony, hotel security, cameras everywhere. If a *rougarou* does make it up there somehow, we'll make history."

Quinn thanked Larue and they said goodnight.

Danni still hadn't come back.

He walked out to the shop and saw that she was staring at her front window from the back. Her displays were always excellent. She knew where to shop and where to find the right pieces that made everything perfect. He slipped his arms around her waist and rested his chin on the top of her head.

"We'll find out what's going on," he told her.

"The cane," she murmured. "The story goes that Count D'Oro had his own wizard, and the silver grip wolf's head on his cane was magical. That it gave him the power to deflect Melissa DeVane's curse and become the *rougarou*."

"We talked about that. I don't think we can find the old cane in the swamp, Danni."

She shook her head. "I don't think the cane is in the swamp. I think someone had it hidden away. And maybe someone else has found it, believing they have the power of the *rougarou*."

"That's a lot of maybes. For now, it's kind of late. Bed?"

She turned in his arms with a smile, then checked the door and called to Wolf. "Hey, boy. Time to guard the hallway."

The dog barked his approval.

Danni hurried ahead and Quinn followed her up the stairs. Wolf curled up on his bed in the hallway. When Quinn entered the room, he found that Danni had laid a trail of her clothing from the doorway to the shower.

He smiled.

And he followed.

The curtain was drawn. Steam filled the bathroom. She stood in the shower. He couldn't help thinking that she could have been a mermaid, or a siren, smiling with the kind of light in her eyes that was sure to drive a man mad. He allowed his gaze to fall upon her.

"Did you need a written invitation?" she asked.

He stripped, stepped into the shower, and drew her into his arms. Warm water beats pulsated on his skin. The surge of steam was both relaxing and invigorating, the feel of her body crushing against his overwhelming. He would never tire of feeling her against him. The wonder in her eyes always seemed so fresh, her smiles evocative. The taste of her lips part of a fantasy, and every time he kissed her he felt a rush of arousal.

Her fingers slid down his back, then moved to his chest.

He reached behind her, cupping her buttocks, and lifting her to him, their every point of contact now an erogenous zone.

He kissed her again.

This time more passionate.

"Shampoo in the tub," she whispered to him.

The words made no sense.

"Slip, fall, break body parts," Danni whispered. "Not as much fun."

Now he understood, and he lifted her over the rim of the tub, following her out quickly himself. Not to lose the moment, he kissed her again, and they became engaged in twined lips and stroking hands.

"Towel rack," Quinn said.

"What?"

"Towel rack. Big bruise on the back, maybe your head against the wall. A concussion. Not as much fun."

They both laughed.

Danni threw open the bedroom door and they made a beeline for the sheets, shivering.

"It's cold out here," she said.

Quinn landed on the bed at her side. "Not to add more bad and trite lines to the wonderful foreplay I've initiated," he kissed her shoulder. "But give me a chance and I'll warm you up."

Safe from falling, tripping, or breaking bones, he wrapped his arms around her, covered her with the length of his body, and eased himself slowly down. She quickly rose against him, seeking the same, kissing his flesh, teasing him, light brushes, far more serious touches that escalated him to a place where the world existed in the physical sense of the two of them, and nothing else.

Later, lying beside her, Quinn thought that life could be

strange indeed. He thought about the wasted years gone before. He hadn't deserved a second chance, but had gotten one anyway. Danni was a part of that second chance. They might not ever really understand their role in the world as it had fallen to them. Maybe Angus had never really understood himself. But Danni was his lifeline now.

Whatever happened, they had one another.

He smiled.

Trite and a bad pickup line. But true.

As long as he had her, the world could send him anything.

Wolf began to bark, then the dog slammed himself against the bedroom door.

Quinn jumped from the bed, drew on his jeans, and reached to the bedside table for the SIG Sauer P226 that Jake Larue had given him last Christmas.

Danni was leaping out of bed, scrambling for clothing too.

"Stay here," he told her. "My old Glock is in the top drawer. Get it."

He hurried out of the room.

Wolf waited in the hall. Bo Ray and Billie were running down the stairs.

"Hold off," Quinn said.

"Following you," Billie said. "Bo Ray, get in with Danni."

The look he tossed Quinn was to remind him that Billie had worked with Angus for years before a young upstart like Quinn had come along.

Wolf led the way to the ground floor and the courtyard entrance. Quinn opened the door and Wolf rushed out, barking furiously. Quinn stood perfectly still. Whoever had been there was gone. And whoever had been there had been blessed with the capability of jumping high fences, as the gate that led out to Royal Street was still latched tightly.

"Quinn," Billie said. "Over here."

He walked to the courtyard entry for the kitchen. There, by the door, were what appeared to be footprints of some large bipedal creature.

Billie hunkered down and touched the substance creating the prints, then looked up at Quinn.

They both knew what it was.

Blood.

* * * *

Danni poured coffee as she listened to Quinn.

It had been just a few minutes after 6:00 a.m. when Wolf, Billie, and Quinn came back into the house, too late to bother trying to get back to sleep.

Quinn called Larue.

No, he didn't want a major investigation. No, he didn't believe that the Royal Street house had been besieged by a league of *rougarous*. He didn't want a big deal made out of it. No sirens blazing.

"But I want to know what that blood substance is, so send a tech over," he told Larue. "Whatever is going on, they think they're going to scare Danni and me away. That's what that was all about. *Rougarou* or not—whatever, whoever, they didn't want to mess with Wolf. We're in good shape here, and whoever came by didn't actually try to get in. Just get me a tech to look at the substance."

He listened, thanked Larue, hung up, and came for the coffee pot.

"They'll have somebody here in a few minutes."

"They have anything yet on Byron Grayson?" Danni asked.

Quinn shook his head. "Go figure. A major office building in the Central Business District and no one saw a thing. I'm heading out to the swamp today. I want you—"

"Quinn, you can't worry about me all the time. That's not the way this works." She stood on her toes to plant a quick kiss on his lips. "However, today, you don't have to worry about me. Natasha and I are heading to the library. We're going to find out what's happened over the years." She was quiet a minute and then said, "There are dozens of theories but in Salem, Massachusetts, during the witch hysteria, a strong theory was that people let their hatred take hold, and a lot of that hatred had to do with people wanting prime land. Accuse a neighbor and the land was taken and then it went up for sale. None of that came about this time until David and Julian opened their business. I'm going to see who is doing what."

"Byron Grayson wanted the land," Quinn told her. "And Grayson has gone missing."

"Be careful," she said.

He gave her what should have been a quick kiss good-bye for the day.

She caught the anguish in his eyes and the kiss became something deeper.

A loud "ahem" made them break apart and laugh.

Bo Ray had apparently followed Billie in, because he said, "See, when life is good, you just don't think the way some others might. That came out wrong. That doesn't mean that all single people are sex fiends. I just...okay. Bo Ray, time to just shut up and get your foot out of your mouth."

Quinn looked at Bo Ray and shook his head with amusement. "Keep in touch all day, everyone."

Billie nodded.

"Go," Danni told Quinn. "You two have coffee. Enjoy your breakfast. I'm going to take that display down before I take off with Natasha."

Quinn exited out the kitchen door to the courtyard and the garage. He paused there, looking back at her. She smiled. He nodded and kept going. Danni headed down the hallway and into the store. Moving a few props, she reached the store side of her left facing display window. The mannequin wasn't heavy, just a little awkward. She picked it up first and set it down, staring at the creation. It was damned good. She'd bought it from a friend in Louisiana's booming film business.

The eyes almost seemed to follow her.

She wagged a finger at the mannequin. "Sick murderer, playing on legend. How could you kill that beautiful young woman who never hurt a soul? Or kill anyone. Look at the legacy you've left."

Crawling back into the window, she hurriedly gathered the rest of the items that had made up the display, tossing them into the shop. Then she looked around, trying to decide what she was going to put up in place of the display on Count D'Oro and the *rougarou*.

Billie came into the shop.

"Egyptian," she announced. "We have that mannequin of Cleopatra. We can add a lot of the local jewelry. There's a really beautiful ankh and then, to the side, we can add in a display of those fleur-de-lis pendants. Not Egyptian per se, but for now it will do."

"Aye, lass, got it. I'll need Bo Ray to help."

He turned and left her, heading back down the hallway.

The mannequin of Count D'Oro suddenly fell over.

The cane rolled across the floor and landed at Danni's feet, the silver wolf's head seeming to stare up at her. For a moment, she froze. The way the mannequin had landed, it seemed to be staring at her too. She trembled despite herself, then walked over and glared down at the mannequin, kicking the cane to the side.

"We will end this," she said with determination.

And it almost seemed like the mannequin disagreed.

Challenging her to do so.

Chapter 5

Quinn met up with Detectives Beauchamp and Deerfield and they headed out on a police boat, stopping by properties in Honey Swamp, briefly speaking to those they found along the way. Everyone seemed to think that the *rougarou* had awakened, so they were all staying armed and close to home.

"I'm going to have a bunch of shot-up tourists on my hands soon enough," Deerfield said, looking a bit like a disgruntled bulldog.

They saved Selena Duarte for the next to the last and planned on visiting Julian Henri's property last. Quinn hopped up on the dock at Selena Duarte's rustic wood home on the water. He knocked at the door several times, peered in the window, and knocked again.

No answer.

He headed back down to the dock to speak with Beauchamp and Deerfield.

"She's not there," he said.

"Selena's there," Deerfield said. "She's just being an old pain in the ass."

Deerfield hopped to the dock and left Beauchamp and Quinn to tie up the boat.

"Selena, you ornery cuss. It's Detective Deerfield. Open the damned door."

To Quinn's surprise, the door opened.

Selena Duarte was white haired and wrinkled to the nines, and she appeared to be older than the earth itself.

"What the hell you doing out here, bothering an old woman? You know damned well I ain't guilty of a damned thing. What, you think I could even wield some kind of a weapon hard enough to do in a big man or a woman for that matter? And you think I got good teeth all of a sudden? My dentures barely bite through butter."

"Not out here to accuse you of anything, Selena. We came here to find out if you might have seen anything," Beauchamp told her.

She pointed at Quinn. "What you doing out here, football-blow-it-all boy? Heard you went military, cop, and then P.I. in New Orleans. You're a far cry from the city, Quinn. You know nothing about these swamps."

"I did grow up in the area, Mrs. Duarte. I've been out here often enough," Quinn said.

She sniffed. "So they called you in, huh? Thinking that you could catch the *rougarou*. They're wrong. The *rougarou* belongs to the swamp. When the *rougarou* is hungry, people are going to die. That's all there is to it. When the *rougarou* has had his share of killing, then it will all stop. And that's the way it is. You go work your mumbo-jumbo in the city, young man." She pointed a long, bony finger at Quinn. "You watch your step. The *rougarou* knows about you."

"Is that a threat, Mrs. Duarte?" Quinn asked. "If so, the *rougarou* will have to get in line."

She sniffed loudly and looked at Dirk Deerfield. "We both know, don't we, Dirk? They didn't catch no one last time, and they're not going to catch anyone this time. The *rougarou* will do what the *rougarou* wants."

"Just like the honey badger," Beauchamp murmured.

Selena turned her sharp gaze on Beauchamp. "That some kind of a joke, boy?"

"No, ma'am."

"Selena," Deerfield said. "All I want to know is have you seen anything?"

"Yeah, I seen something. I seen it moving through the thick trees. It's big. Can't say as I saw the face clearly, but seems to me I kind of saw it in my eyes. Teeth like you wouldn't believe. Ugly face, ugly as sin. I heard something in the back, looked out there, and saw it running through the trees. I shut my door and lit a few candles on my altar. I got out my poor dead husband's shotgun and I sat there with it all night, though I knew if the *rougarou* wanted me, the shotgun wouldn't matter none. But, like last time, the *rougarou* isn't after an old woman who spent her life working and just wants to be left alone." Selena looked at Deerfield. "The *rougarou* is after the innocent and the sinners. None of us in between folk. You mark my words, you'll find out those people you ain't identified yet were sinners, or maybe a priest and a nun. Don't know which. But there will be somethin' about them."

"Selena, which way was the *rougarou* running?" Quinn asked her.

"Away from my place, heading for the highway. Maybe he hitchhiked his way into New Orleans. What do you think? Maybe he can fly. Don't know, don't care. I intend to keep to myself, like always."

"Selena, if you see or hear anything, anything at all," Deerfield began.

"What? I'm going to call you? I ain't got no phone out here, Dirk. No cell phone, no house phone. Maybe I can send up some smoke signals."

And she laughed.

"I'll be back by," Deerfield promised.

"You be careful, Dirk Deerfield. You're just the kind of man the *rougarou* may want."

"Mrs. Duarte," Beauchamp said politely, "you really are mean as dirt."

"You go on now. All of you. Ain't nothing here for you. You're spinning wheels, just spinning wheels. The *rougarou* will take what it wants, and if you leave it alone, the damned thing will go back to sleep and by the time it comes back again, I'll be dust and ash in the cemetery. Go on. Git."

Quinn was certain that if she'd been holding a shotgun, she would have pointed it at them. He turned and headed down the dock with the other two men.

But Beauchamp couldn't let it go and turned back. "You're sad, Selena Duarte. A sad old sack of a woman. Sorry to say, I'll probably be the one picking up your bones when you die, holed up in your shack all alone, without anyone to give a damn."

Selena stared after them, startled and in silence.

"Unless the *rougarou* gets you first," Beauchamp muttered.

They continued to the boat.

Little else to do.

* * * *

"Danni?"

She was down in the "basement" of the shop, in her father's office, sifting through page after page in his book, hoping for another reference to the *rougarou*.

The voice was Jake Larue's.

"I'm down here," she called out.

Larue descended the stairs and said, "You're not alone down here, are you?"

"Hardly."

Wolf lay at her feet.

"Someone is playing tricks on us," he said. "Those footprints at your place, the substance. It's blood. Human. It came from the second victim, the young woman Quinn found in the swamp. I'm beginning to wonder if there is a *rougarou* running around."

"A very athletic *rougarou*," Danni said. "How does the creature make its way into the city? Does it have a chauffeur? In which case, we're still looking for a living, breathing man. Has forensics determined the type of blood that was found in Byron Grayson's office?"

"They're still trying, coming up with gator, raccoon, fox, and wild boar."

"A mixture?"

"Hard to analyze, or so I've been told."

"Has anyone found Byron Grayson?"

"No sign of him."

"But," she asked, her words slow, "no more bodies, right?"

"No more bodies. I tried to get Quinn. He must be out of phone range. I just wanted to tell you to make sure that you were careful. Someone, or something, was in your courtyard."

"I have Wolf," she said. "But I promise, I'll be careful."

He said good-bye and she returned her attention to the book. But no answers were there. She closed the cover, called to Wolf, and locked up the basement. Heading up to the shop, she told Billie she was going to the library. Wolf would have to stay at the house.

She also shared what Larue had told her with Billie.

"I'll be on the lookout. And Wolf is the best alarm system in the world. He's got an instinct that puts you and Quinn to shame," he added with a grin.

"Yes, he does. Anything from Natasha or Father Ryan?"

"Natasha called a bit ago. She's put some feelers out among

her community. People are scared. Most believe that there is a monster out there, *rougarou* or other."

"And Father Ryan?"

"He said that he's checking into local records. No word among his parishioners that anyone knows anything about what's been happening."

"I'll be at the library on Loyola," she said.

She headed into the courtyard and across to the garage. Twenty minutes later, she was sitting in the public library. The librarian had been a tremendous help, supplying her with stack upon stack of information dealing with the Wolfman murders of twenty years ago. She was deep into her reading when she jumped, startled to see that someone had taken a seat in front of her.

Father Ryan.

She let out a sigh and sat back, smiling. "You startled me."

"What have you found?" he asked her.

"Did you ever hear of or know a man named Jacob Devereaux?"

"Sure. He was a realtor in town. Died years ago, though."

"Did you know that he was interviewed about the murder of Genevieve LaCoste?"

"I did. He was a frequent visitor to her shop, if I recall. The supposition at the time was that he had a crush on her. But he also had an alibi. There was nothing that suggested he'd pulled off the crime. The police were looking everywhere. I think the belief at the time was that the murderer had been transient, and that he'd moved on. Either that, or he was a *rougarou*, and his appetite for blood had been sated."

"This guy didn't happen to be a parishioner of yours, did he?" Danni asked hopefully.

He shook his head.

"They haven't found Byron Grayson," she told him. "All

they found was a pool of mixed up blood in his office. What if he's out in the swamp? What if he's gone a little crazy, wanting to buy property, determined to make it so bad for David and Julian that they have to sell?"

"Danni, if you brought this theory into a court of law, they'd laugh at you."

"I know, but you said Jacob Devereaux was dead. Here's the thing. Go back to the beginning. Count D'Oro brutally killed Melissa DeVane because he wanted her and her magic. More powerful than the magic his own wizard possessed, even though the magic of his supposed wizard was strong enough to keep him alive as a monster. Let's say that twenty years ago, this Jacob Devereaux was in love with Genevieve LaCoste, and she wanted nothing to do with him. He knew about the legend, maybe he even knew about the power that was supposed to be in Count D'Oro's cane. Somehow he knew where the cane could be found. Once he had the cane, he thought he was all-powerful. So he killed the young women and then he died."

Father Ryan rose and walked over to the counter and the helpful librarian. A few minutes later, the librarian produced an old book. Father Ryan didn't come back to the table. He flipped through the book, returned it to the librarian, then came over to where Danni was sitting.

"Jacob Devereaux died twenty years ago. A month after the last murder," he said. "Now, I warn you, that doesn't prove anything."

"I still think we should call Quinn and Larue. Someone who was in love with that young woman, who was found in the swamp, might be worth investigating."

"Danni, they haven't identified her. How are they going to find someone who might have been in love with her? And the first person killed was a man."

"Yeah, I know," Danni said, frustrated.

Her phone rang. She glanced at the caller ID.

Quinn.

"You're all right," she said, answering.

"Yeah, and you?"

"I'm with Father Ryan." She smiled across the table at the priest.

"I thought I should check in," Quinn said. "Also, we have an ID on the man whose body was discovered first. Abel Denham. New Englander. A realtor, planning on relocating to Southern Louisiana."

"Realtor?" She looked at Father Ryan. "Quinn, I think that's it. He might have been out there looking at property. Byron Grayson remains missing, but he might be out there too. In that swamp." She gripped the phone tighter. "Killing people."

"We're at Julian's property now, by the boat slip. It's the departure point for their tours. I'll call you back if I find anything. What's up on your end?"

"Realtors. Lots of realtors," Danni said firmly. "Are you with the Pearl River police? Ask Detective Deerfield if he remembers interviewing a man named Jacob Devereaux. He was suspected to have had a crush, some kind of longing, for Genevieve LaCoste. If so, this could all tie in."

"Will do," Quinn said. "Stay safe, okay?"

"Absolutely," she promised, ending the call.

She repeated the conversation to Father Ryan, who stood. "I'll head up to the Garden District and see what people can remember about Genevieve."

"How are you going to do that?"

"Public record. I'll find out who's still in the same area and then I'll knock on some doors."

"And they'll just let you in?"

He smiled and shrugged. "This collar can open a lot of doors. Keep in contact."

She promised that she would and he left. For several seconds, Danni drummed her fingers on the table. Then she picked up her phone and called Larue.

He answered her second ring.

"I was just thinking," she said. "Does anyone know yet why Abel Denham was relocating to New Orleans?"

"I guess he fell in love with the city. People do," Larue said.

"We need to find out why he was relocating, Jake." She hesitated. "I believe it was because of a young woman. He was coming here to be with someone, because she'd moved to New Orleans. Maybe his girlfriend was a student or a teacher. Maybe she was coming down to work at or go to one of the colleges. I don't know. But I think that's a possibility."

"Okay, we'll move in that direction," he said. "We'd figured the victims had been random."

"Twenty years ago, only young women were killed. And look into anything you can find about Jacob Devereaux."

"He's been dead for years."

"Humor me."

"I'll do my best."

They hung up and Danni stood. Quinn and Father Ryan had been by Victoria Miller's tour company headquarters, but she hadn't. She didn't know Victoria Miller. Maybe it was time to check her out.

She thanked the librarian, headed to her car, then back to the French Quarter. She didn't want to be seen at the shop, so she parked at the public lot by the river, then headed to Crescent City Sites, intent on meeting Victoria Miller herself. The woman wasn't a realtor, but she had tried to buy Julian Henri's property on the swamp.

The front doors were open to the street, as were those of many businesses in the area. The tour desk was just about eight feet back from the entry, but there wasn't anyone manning it.

Danni wandered in. There was an office in the back. Perhaps the woman was there. Before she could go in, she heard a voice whispering with anger.

"You were supposed to be gone. I paid you good money. You were supposed to be gone."

"Hey, I like the city. No one but that idiot knows who I am."

As Danni stood there, another man came in from the street. He had an air of authority about him, as if he belonged there. He paused, aware of the whispered conversation too.

"Can I help you?" he asked her.

"Yes, I'm actually living in the city," she said. "But there's so much I haven't seen and so much I don't know. I was thinking of taking some tours."

She spoke softly, hoping to hear more of the conversation going on in the office, but that wasn't to be the case.

A man emerged from the back.

He appeared to be about thirty with shaggy, unkempt hair, wearing dungarees and a faded plaid shirt. He looked at Danni, caught her eye, smiled, and then exited the front doors.

"I'm Gene Andre," the man who had first come in said, stepping behind the desk. "I'd be delighted to help you. What are you thinking? French Quarter, Garden District, ghost tour, vampire tour. You name it, we do it all. And, of course, all our guides are completely licensed. We're good here in New Orleans. Lots of stories that may or may not be true, but the city asks that we have our facts right."

Before she could reply, a woman came bursting out of the office.

Attractive, smartly dressed, and furious.

"Don't talk to her, Andre. I know who she is. That's Danielle Cafferty. She's with that bull-sized P.I., Quinn. She's here to try and make it look like we're guilty in all this somehow.

Get out, Cafferty. Get out now, before I call the police and issue a restraining order against you and Quinn for harassment."

"I was really interested in your tours." Danni lifted her hands. "But that's okay. I'm gone."

She left the office quickly, thinking that her ruse hadn't gone well. On the street, she paused for a minute. A prickling sensation seemed to rip along her spine. She turned quickly and saw that the man who'd been arguing with Victoria was just across the street, by the old Jax Brewery.

He was studying her.

He realized that she saw him, then hurried off.

* * * *

Julian Henri met Quinn and the Pearl River detectives at his property.

A new wooden sign with the words *Legends Tours* rose high on a pair of wooden piles at the side of the property, visible from the swamp and from the old gravel road that led in from the main highway.

"This is it," Julian said. "And why the hell anyone would want it, I'm not sure."

He opened the front door and led them in.

There was a large living area filled with comfortable chairs and a sofa. Just beyond, a counter with an open area led into a functional kitchen where there was a large coffee pot and a bowl with offerings of various kinds of snack bars.

"We thought we had it just right," Julian said. "A bus to bring people out here, and then they could mill around a bit while we gave them some history and allowed for anyone who wanted to head here by their own transportation to arrive. We tried to make it homey and comfortable. We wanted it to be like you were on an adventure with friends."

"Nice," Quinn murmured. "And back there?" he asked, pointing down a hall.

"Two bedrooms. If we had to, or needed to, for any reason, we could stay out here." He shrugged. "I grew up in this house. My parents had the left room. I had the one on the right. The back door leads to the docks."

"I'll look at the rooms," Beauchamp said.

"I'll take the dock," Deerfield said.

"I'll just look at everything," Quinn said.

"Please, anywhere, anything," Julian told them.

While Beauchamp was in the one bedroom, Quinn headed to the next, which must have been Julian Henri's parents' room. The walls were covered with bookcases and hundreds of books. He looked them over. Classics, manuals, and a lot of contemporary novels. Staring at the shelves, he saw that the older Henri had kept order too. Hunting, fishing, and how-to books in one area. Dickens, Poe, Lovecraft, Thoreau, and more together in another. There was also a shelf for authors associated with Louisiana in one way or another. Eudora Welty, Truman Capote, Tennessee Williams, and more. But oddly, stuck between *In Cold Blood* and *A Streetcar Named Desire* was a book with no title and a worn leather cover.

He reached for the book and quickly realized that it was Julian Henri's father's journal.

He flipped through the pages, seeing all kinds of entries. Bass-fishing tournament, Julian's grade school play. Mardi Gras notations. Years of a father's plans for his wife and child and himself. He decided to concentrate on entries that had been written twenty years ago.

I told the bastard I wouldn't sell. He kept insisting that I could have a better life elsewhere. I told him I'm a swamp man. He said it was no life for a child. I told him my child was brilliant and would do what he wanted, when he wanted. Bad taste left in my mouth.

Quinn flipped through a few more pages.

They found her today in the swamp. That beautiful, beautiful girl. I told them that they needed to check out Jacob Devereaux. He was the most insistent son-of-a-bitch I've ever met. I was in the city, in her shop one day, and I caught him doing the same thing with her, insisting that her boyfriend was a louse and that she needed to be with him.

A day later another entry was also about the murder and Jacob Devereaux.

He was here again. Told me that if the murders continued, my place would be worthless. I should sell now. I threw him out. Then, later in the day, I wanted to take a stroll. Went to get the old cane with the beautiful silver wolf's head grip. It was gone. I'll be damned if the bastard didn't steal it. I kept it right by the door.

* * * *

As Danni headed to her car, her phone rang.

She glanced at the caller ID and saw that it was Natasha and answered. "You've got something?"

"Maybe, maybe not. I talked to Father Ryan about your conversation in the library. He told me that you were curious about that long ago realtor, Jacob Devereaux. An old-timer friend of mine came in the store and we started talking. He's convinced there is a *rougarou*, by the way, but here's the thing. He knew Devereaux. Said the man was slimy as motor oil. Had money, and thought that meant he could buy any woman he wanted. Said he slept with who he wanted, when he wanted. And get this, Danni, he was sure that Devereaux had a child out of wedlock. Didn't know with who or what the kid's name might have been, but he's convinced that the child existed."

Danni quickly filled in the gaps, then added, "Let's say that Jacob Devereaux wasn't just a slimy dick, he was also a murderer. How better to get rid of people than to kill them in the swamps as a *rougarou*. He dies, the murders stop. But his child would now be about twenty."

"Or older," Natasha said.

Danni let out her breath. "I know it's nothing but theory. But it's not a bad one. Devereaux is a human monster. A killer. He has a child out of wedlock, murders the women he can't get, like beautiful Genevieve. He has a child who comes back—"

Her phone signaled that another call was coming through.

"Hang on," she said to Natasha. "Larue is calling. I've got to go. I'll call you later."

She switched lines, still walking back to the car park by the river.

"Danni, you're psychic," Larue told her. "I checked into our first victim. He did come here because of his girlfriend. She's due to start a teaching position at the end of the month and hasn't been seen in the last few days. They haven't been reported missing because they were both moving. We're working on finding out if our second victim *is* Mandy Matheson, Abel Denham's girlfriend. I'll call as soon as I have anything else. I'm working on getting the information to Quinn right now."

"Thanks, Jake. Also, I saw a suspicious looking character at Crescent City Sites arguing with Victoria Miller, just before she threw me out. I'm not sure if it's relevant to the case but wanted to let you know." Something about the fight bothered her, though she knew better than to get stuck on any one thing when dealing with a case, so she changed course. "We've been looking for a connection between the murders twenty years ago and the murders now. There was a man back then named Jacob Devereaux. Natasha just told me that Devereaux very likely had a child out of wedlock. Count D'Oro was in love with the Good Witch of Honey Swamp. She died, along with others. Devereaux had a thing for Genevieve LaCoste, and she was the last to die on the next go-around."

"We'll look into it all, Danni," Larue said. "I'll get with Quinn and the Pearl River detectives."

"Thanks."

She ended the call and slipped her key into the lock of her car. Movement from behind caught her attention. She whirled to see the unkempt man from Crescent City Sites. The very one she'd just mentioned to Jake. But that thought was short lived.

Something hard slammed into the side of her head.

And the world went dark.

* * * *

Quinn brought the journal to Dirk Deerfield and showed him the entries.

"You remember this man Devereaux?" he asked.

"Of course, I remember him. We never had anything on him, though. At the time when Genevieve would have been killed, he had an alibi. A prostitute in the Quarter swore that he'd been with her. Weak alibi, but an alibi. I couldn't charge the bastard, then he up and died. The murders stopped about a month before his death. Peter Henri, Julian's dad, had a thing for Devereaux. Hated him long before any of the murders in the swamp started. Everyone here was accusing everyone else. Old Selena claimed that the *rougarou* did it. And when it came up again, how the hell do you blame a man who is dead for murdering people?"

"Someone has the cane," Quinn said. "Someone sick enough to kill a lot of people. I want to check out what's going on in the city."

He put a call through to Larue.

As soon as he had the detective on the line, he told him what he had found.

"Danni just called me about Devereaux," Larue told him.

"How do I connect a realtor who has been dead for twenty years with a realtor who was moving down to New Orleans? None of this really makes any sense." Quinn couldn't help but have the same thoughts. "There was also a mystery man at the Crescent City Sites tour office, not happy with Victoria. Danni heard them arguing before she was thrown out. She's also convinced that it somehow goes back to men who can't get the women they want."

In other words, they had a mess on their hands.

"Hey," Beauchamp called out. "Get down here."

"I'll call you back," Quinn said and ended the call.

He'd been in the house with Julian. Beauchamp and Deerfield were down at the docks. Julian looked at him with alarm. Quinn brushed past him and hurried to the docks. Beauchamp had walked into the high grasses at the shoreline.

"Third victim," Beauchamp shouted. "Might be Byron Grayson."

Quinn walked to the water. There was a body in the swamp. The head was bashed in, the throat was gone. He'd been there for a while as the crabs had been busy.

He suspected Beauchamp was right.

And Byron Grayson wasn't under suspicion anymore.

"Get Doc Melloni out here," Deerfield said.

* * * *

The first thing Danni became aware of when she came to was the blinding pain in her head. She was going to have a lump the size of Texas on her skull. The next thing she realized was that she was tied and gagged, lying in the trunk of a moving car. Quinn's training came to her quickly. Kick out the back lights. She struggled and twisted and finally got her legs in position.

She kicked hard.

And was rewarded with the sound of broken glass.

She'd done it.

The car jerked to a stop.

The trunk opened.

"Clever little witch, aren't you. Doesn't matter much. We're here."

He reached into the car and with a startling strength, lifted her out.

She saw nothing but trees and bushes, but smelled the air.

They were at a swamp.

Honey Swamp, she imagined.

She struggled like crazy against the man carrying her. They were leaving the dirt road, moving closer to the water.

"Stop it," he said. "I'm not trying to hurt you."

Really?

He had a strange way of showing it.

"You are the witch," he said. "The Good Witch of Honey Swamp. They said that you were dangerous. I didn't understand until I saw you. But it's you. All good and noble, tempting men as if you were a naked siren on the high seas. Oh, no, I don't want to hurt you. The *rougarou* has a very special plan for you."

The *rougarou?*

He carried her to an old, dilapidated shack close to the water, hidden in a thicket of trees. He shoved open the door with a foot. There was a cot on the floor and he eased her down to it.

"The *rougarou* is coming," he told her.

And he left, closing the door behind him.

Then she saw it.

Leaning against one wall.

A cane.

With a silver wolf's head for the grip.

Chapter 6

Quinn called Larue back as Doc Melloni supervised the initial assessment of the body and had it fished from the water.

"The poor bastard," Larue said over the phone. "I guess I'll get on out there. I've got people working on all the angles we discussed. Hey, by the way, I've been trying to get Danni back on the phone. Do you know where she is?"

Quinn frowned. "When did you last speak with her?"

"About an hour ago. Maybe a little more."

"I'm hanging up and going to try to reach her."

He did and Danni didn't answer. He tried the shop, then Natasha and Father Ryan. Naturally, he sent them all into a panic. Something he too was beginning to feel.

He thought back to the events of the day, searching for any red flags, and called Larue. "Get to Crescent City Sites." It was probably nothing, but it was all they had. "Find out who that mystery man was. Drag Victoria in for questioning if you have to, but get some answers." Fear sank in his stomach. "I can't find Danni."

"I'm on it," Larue told him.

Quinn jumped down to the docks. Fear gripped him like a vise.

Deerfield came over to him.

"I can't find Danni Cafferty," he told the cop. "And I've got a bad feeling."

"You don't have to stay here. Get back to the city."

Quinn stood. "No. If he's got her, he's going to bring her out here, somewhere."

"Maybe you're panicking unnecessarily."

He shook his head. "Danni wouldn't be unreachable if she were all right." She carried her phone at all times. "He's got her and she's out here. And I'm going to find her."

"This swamp is enormous. We'll have to call out every officer we have."

Quinn looked at the police cruiser. "I need your boat."

"You got it. What are you going to do? I'll go with you."

"You stay here. I'll take the boat."

"I'll get Beauchamp out searching, too."

"There's one person I have to talk to, and I will get answers from her," Quinn said.

He left Deerfield and the commotion with the body and headed out. Selena Duarte must have heard the boat returning. She stuck her head out and then disappeared, slamming the door.

Quinn's phone rang as he jumped up on the dock.

It was Larue.

"Found her car, Quinn, parked by the river. Her cell phone was on the asphalt by the driver's side." Only years of training kept him from total panic.

"What about Victoria Miller and that boyfriend of hers?" Quinn asked.

Larue seemed to hesitate a moment.

"We can't find them, Quinn. The business is all locked up. I've got every cop in the city looking for them."

Quinn raced toward Selena Duarte's front door and banged on it. "You can answer the door or I'll break it down."

"They'll fire you," she called back.

"I'm not a cop, and I don't give a damn if they arrest me. You will let me in right now. And you will tell me what's going on out here."

No reply.

He slammed his shoulder hard against the door.

Wood reverberated.

Two more times and he'd have the damn thing open.

"Stop," Selena called out from inside.

The door opened and she stood there with a shotgun in her hand.

"Put that damned gun down," Quinn said.

She stared at him a moment and then lowered the weapon. "Ain't no shells in it anyway. Or maybe I would've shot ya."

"I need your help," he told her.

"I'm not the *rougarou*," she said.

His phone rang.

Larue.

No choice, he had to answer.

"Where are you?" Larue asked.

"Getting answers," Quinn said.

"I spoke to those two young girls again, the ones who saw the *rougarou* on their balcony. Jane Eagle and Lana Adair. I asked them about men being inappropriate, urging them to go out. Seems some young guy at a bar on Bourbon Street got really obnoxious. He insisted that they come with him. The bouncer at the bar is a huge guy, a friend of the cops in the Quarter. The girls came to him, but before he could do anything the guy disappeared."

"Thanks," Quinn said. "Gotta go. Doesn't matter too much who it is now. I've just got to find Danni."

"We've got officers streaming into the swamp, Quinn."

"They won't be in time. I've got to go."

He hung up. "Selena, talk to me. Time is running out."

"I don't help the *rougarou*. I just know that it's out there."

"Whoever, whatever it is, it has a friend of mine. And I will kill or die in the process, but I will do everything I can to find her. Now, are you going to help me?"

* * * *

Danni worked as hard as she could at the ropes that were binding her. She managed to free the gag from her mouth, but doubted screaming was going to do her any good. She had to stay calm and collected, which was difficult. At any moment, someone could walk in, bash her head in, then rip her throat out. Quinn was out here, but Honey Swamp was twenty miles long and seven miles wide, one of the most pristine river swamps in the country. Lots of isolated places. It was so crazy. The man who'd taken her was definitely crazy. But he wasn't the *rougarou*. Instead, someone else was coming. And why had her captor seen her as Melissa DeVane? Because of the shop? Because of what she and Quinn did, searching down objects? And there was the cane across the shack. Refurbished, certainly. Its length appeared to be ebony, making the silver of the wolf's head all the more shiny. She winced, thinking that the head of the cane might have been the object used to smash in the victims' heads.

She kept struggling, while thoughts raced through her mind. Who could have done all this? Was the man who'd kidnapped her the bastard child of Jacob Devereaux? If so, why isn't he the *rougarou*? Wouldn't he have taken on that role, rather than leaving it to someone else?

There was always a reason for murder.

Jacob Devereaux had obviously been a sick narcissist, determined to kill Genevieve LaCoste because she wanted nothing to do with him. But this time it had been a man who'd been killed first, then his girlfriend. Had someone been in love and killed his rival, then the woman who'd turned him down?

She kept working on her bindings.

Her hands came free.

She sat up and drew her legs close, working desperately on the knots at her ankles, which were tight. But she was determined. She leapt to her feet, ready to reach for the cane and run.

The door to the shack blew open.

And there it stood.

The *rougarou*.

Immense, covered in some kind of pelt, with a giant wolf's head.

Before she could move, it picked up the cane.

And came toward her.

* * * *

"What is it that you've seen, Selena? Damn it, you have to tell me," Quinn demanded.

"I told you, I'm not the *rougarou*. And if I say anything, the *rougarou* will kill me. I may be old, but I don't want to go that way."

"Selena, I'm going to hurt you worse than any *rougarou*."

"You wouldn't."

"Try me. And why do you think that the *rougarou* will kill you for talking? How will the *rougarou* know that you even talked to me?"

She was silent for an unbearable moment, gnawing on her

lip. "He left me a message. In the mud. I came out to hang laundry and it was there, in the yard. A big dug-out sign that said *Silence is golden. Silence is life.* I know it was from the *rougarou.*"

The same kind of message that had threatened David Fagin.

He decided to try kindness and softened his tone. "You tell me what you know and I'll see to it that you're safe from the *rougarou* forever."

"I wish I believed you," she said.

"Believe me. The *rougarou* dies today."

"I know just about where he lives," Selena said. "Or where I think he lives."

"Near here?"

She hesitated. "I've seen him come and go. When I've looked through the trees, I've seen him. Come out with me, in back. I'll show you where."

"Let's go," Quinn said.

* * * *

The *rougarou* picked up the cane and pointed it toward Danni.

She stayed dead still. There was no way to escape. And the thing didn't speak. It just stood there, impossibly tall with its giant wolf's head, neck, and ears. A mask, of course. A man beneath.

"You will be dead," she said. "I swear it."

The man who'd taken her captive appeared from behind the *rougarou.* "You think you can curse the *rougarou.* I knew that you were the reincarnation of the witch. I knew it."

"I don't curse people and I'm not a witch," she said. "But I can tell you that Michael Quinn will be looking for me, and when he finds me, you two are going to pay."

She was sure that she heard the *rougarou* speak beneath his mask, and he seemed angry with the man who'd seized her. Seemed like threatening had bought her time, though how anyone would find her in the swamp, she didn't know.

She pointed at the man who'd seized her, deciding to play a hunch. "You're the illegitimate son of a man named Jacob Devereaux, aren't you?" Her guess got their attention, so she continued. "Why you would want to follow in the footsteps of a father who didn't even recognize your existence, I don't know. And why you would be subservient to another, when you're the son of the last *rougarou*, that's mind boggling."

"You are a witch, definitely a witch!" the man cried. "But I will be the next *rougarou*, whether your idiot friends hire me or not."

One more piece of the puzzle clicked. And with her only goal to keep him talking, she threw another accusation their way. "So is the *rougarou* Victoria? Did she get you to apply for a job with David and Julian so that you could find out more about what they were doing? Were you supposed to try to sabotage their tours? Guess what? You didn't even impress them enough to remember your name."

"Shut up, witch! My name is Jim Novak and they damn well know it. You're just stupid! You're a stupid witch," he said.

The *rougarou* slammed the cane against the man and whispered something that Danni didn't catch.

Novak stepped toward her. She leapt at him, striking, clawing, screaming, using all of her strength. To no avail. He gave her a head-ringing pop atop her head and the world began to spin.

He tossed her over his shoulder and headed outside.

She struggled as he set her down and reached for ropes.

She was being tied to a tree.

In the time that he'd left her before the arrival of the *rougarou*, Jim Novak had been preparing for her death.

She wasn't going to be beaten or ripped to death.

She was going to be burned alive.

* * * *

Selena Duarte brought Quinn out back, to the land side of her Honey Swamp shack, and pointed far to the west.

"Through all those trees," she said. "When I see him, it's in that direction. I've seen him there many times. I don't know what's back there. It's overgrown and dense. And there are potholes and swampy land in between. All kinds of critters. Gators, snakes. They leave the *rougarou* alone. But you may not make it through."

"I'll make it," Quinn told her. "And Selena. Thank you."

He headed in the direction she'd pointed. By his reckoning, there was a lot of marshy land between Selena's, the main swamp, and the road. But there had to be something out there. Some kind of old camp or shack. As he walked, he called Larue and told him where he was and where he was going.

"Find out," he said. "There has to be something around these coordinates. Get some techs on it. Maybe there's a way for cops to get there by a road of some kind before I can make it."

Larue promised he was on it.

Quinn kept walking. Grass tangled around his feet. The mud was ankle-deep. He came upon a patch of bare land by a little pool. A gator, six or seven feet long, lay half in and out of the water.

"Brother, leave me alone and I'll leave you alone," Quinn said.

He skirted the alligator and kept going. Luckily, the beast continued bathing in what remained of the sunlight. He paused, looking ahead. For a moment, he thought that he saw smoke.

Which quickly dissipated.

He blinked but kept going, with a landmark now.

Toward the smoke.

* * * *

"You can't kill me," Danni said. "I'm the Good Witch of Honey Swamp, remember? I can make it rain."

She so startled Jim Novak that, for a moment, he paused and looked up at the sky.

"I call upon the rain," she yelled, feeling ridiculous.

But she had given him pause.

The *rougarou* let out some impatient sound and Novak stepped forward again and lit the dried branches around Danni's feet.

She inhaled an odd smell.

Gasoline.

On the wood.

"I call upon the rain," she shouted again.

And to her amazement, it began to rain.

* * * *

Quinn ran, tripping and stumbling.

To make matters worse, it had begun to rain. Heavy. Almost blinding him. His phone rang. It nearly slipped from his fingers as he answered, still making his way through the mud and muck.

Larue.

"There's an old shack out there. It's been there for years and years. You're not going to believe who originally held the property rights around it."

"Count D'Oro?" Quinn said.

"Bingo. We've got a team heading there as quickly as

possible."

"I'm almost there."

"Quinn, we found Victoria Miller and Gene Andre. I had them brought in. They did hire that guy, Jim Novak is his name, to harass David Fagin and Julian Henri. But they swear that's all they did. They said that he found them and instigated it. He promised he'd find out what David and Julian were up to and that he'd do his best to make their new company miserable. Victoria paid him, but then he wanted more money. Of course, Gene says he was against it from the get-go and wanted to tell us." The doubt was clear in Larue's voice.

"You have both of them?" Quinn asked.

"In custody."

"Thanks. Gotta keep moving."

"Police are on the way."

"They may not be in time."

He hung up and renewed his efforts with a burst of speed. He was pretty sure he knew just who the *rougarou* might be.

And he'd given him plenty of time.

To set a trap.

* * * *

The rain doused the fire, despite the gasoline. But as the sudden deluge eased, Novak stepped forward to light it again.

"I control the wind and the rain," she yelled, praying that the Louisiana weather would not let her down. And, to her relief, it did not. The rain fell harder.

Novak let out a cry of terror.

The *rougarou* seemed undaunted and stepped forward. Tied to the tree, Danni could do nothing. The "creature" drew out a knife. But instead of planting it in her, he severed the ties binding her and drew her from the tree.

Rain kept falling.

The heavy wolf's head cane was raised, ready to smash it down on her head. But a mammoth mud creature burst from the swamp and tackled the *rougarou*.

She blinked away the rain.

The mud creature was Quinn.

Quinn straddled the costumed man, pinning him down, wrenching the cane from him and throwing it away. The *rougarou* struggled for the knife. Quinn backhanded him across the face so hard that his arms fell flat. Danni dived for the knife. She heard a howl. It was Novak, racing for her.

She braced herself, ready to use the knife.

An explosion pierced the air.

Gunfire.

From Quinn's weapon.

Novak was hit in the kneecap. He let out a howl of pain that seemed to tear through the swamp as if a beast had been brought down.

"Get up," Quinn shouted at the *rougarou*.

As he did, the rain eased.

Quinn ripped the mask off.

To reveal Detective Hayden Beauchamp.

Epilogue

Detective Dirk Deerfield was the most stunned that the "*rougarou*" had been his own partner.

He shook his head over and over again.

Quinn felt badly for him. He'd thought his young partner an upright fellow and had been completely duped.

"He asked me about the old case a lot," Deerfield said. "I thought that sometimes it was just to remind me that while I might be the veteran and him the rookie, things had gotten by me. It never occurred to me that he was planning murders in the same way. Murders with the same details."

"How did Beauchamp and Jim Novak meet?" Father Ryan asked. "That has to be one of the most unlikely duos ever."

"It wasn't surprising to me that Jim Novak is slightly crazy," Natasha said. "Ignored by a father who died when he was a child. Not even given his name. His mother didn't want him. He bounced through the system, went through all kinds of foster homes, unwanted. I guess a legacy as a *rougarou* was better than none."

They were all there, Natasha, Father Ryan, Billie, Bo Ray, Danni, Quinn, along with Jake Larue and Dirk Deerfield, gathered at a place called Wicked Times. Beauchamp and Novak had both been arraigned on murder charges. Danni had been cleared from the hospital, since Quinn had insisted she have the knot on her head looked at. Communication between all of them had been somewhat choppy, and they were all still trying to put the pieces together.

It was also supposed to be a social night at Wicked Times. The place was new. It had just opened on Magazine Street, and in an hour or so, Quinn was going to play with the band and he was excited. They had a guy on rhythm guitar named Fats McGinnis, odd name since Fats was a tall, lean, twig of a man, one of the best in the city on guitar.

Danni liked to compare the situation to that of Sherlock Holmes with his violin. But Quinn always assured her he was no Sherlock Holmes.

As if she'd just read his mind, Danni asked, "How did you know? I mean, before you came after him, you knew that the *rougarou* was Hayden Beauchamp."

"Process of elimination, my dear Watson. It was the pieces all of you gave me. Larue was keeping in constant contact. I figured that Jim Novak had something to do with it. But, of course, I could see Novak when I came through the trees. We knew it wasn't Byron Grayson, he was dead in the swamp. When Larue checked with Jane and Lana and found out that, yes, they'd been harassed in a bar on Bourbon, but the guy had disappeared, I figured it had to be Beauchamp. Someone young enough to head out into the bar scene and someone close to the investigation. He knew all the little details of the previous murders that the public might not have known. He'd seen all the crime scene pictures. He knew how the '*rougarou*' had been killing. When we found Byron Grayson in the swamp, Deerfield had us all split up. Naturally, Beauchamp knew that Danni was missing. He knew about my communications with Larue. He had to figure then that Novak had taken Danni for him and that

Novak would think that he had scored the win of the world. Apparently, Beauchamp found the silver wolf's head cane years ago and had become obsessed with the story and its possibilities."

He paused.

"We believe that he actually killed his first victim, an unknown young woman we found buried in the front of the shack, after he found the old property. As you surmised, Danni, people can be sick and cruel and perpetuate heinous crimes without props or legend. But he had the cane. And when he met Novak, he was able to convince him that he was the *rougarou*, and that a *rougarou* always had a man in training, ready to step up to the task. When Beauchamp wanted to get rid of someone or take revenge, he called on Novak, who brought him his victims, and, we believe, did most of the killing. Beauchamp met Mandy Matheson and Abel Denham somewhere in the city when they first arrived. I'm assuming that Beauchamp immediately had a thing for Mandy. When she didn't respond, she was with another man, for God's sake, Beauchamp decided they both deserved to die. But he thought he'd also have a little fun. He knew Victoria Miller. She'd been running tours for a long time. He knew she was furious with David Fagin and Julian Henri. So he sent Novak to befriend them, and then actually got them to pay him to torment Julian Henri.

"When they talked, both Beauchamp and Novak decided that Julian's father had been the bastard who'd somehow caused Jacob Devereaux's death. Devereaux had tried and tried to get ahold of Julian's property, but never did. He'd stolen the cane from Peter Henri, but he'd never managed to dislodge him. Making sure that David and Julian stumbled on the first victim, and then writing a threat in the mud, pretty much ruined their intended business. Though now, knowing that people do tend to like the gruesome, they may be able to start up again."

"We know a lot," Deerfield added, "because Novak is talking a blue streak. He's still convinced that he'll be the *rougarou* one day."

"It's still absolutely amazing that you found me in the middle of a swamp," Danni said.

"More amazing is that you made it rain." Larue grinned.

Father Ryan cleared his throat. "God made it rain. But who knows? Maybe, as the Good Witch that Danni can prove to be, her words went to God's ear."

"It is Southern Louisiana," Danni noted. "It rains all the time."

Everyone at the table turned toward Danni. She did have some powers. Sometimes it was in drawings she made while doodling or when she sleepwalked. This time?

Rain.

"Maybe the legend of the *rougarou* is a little bit true, and maybe the legend of the Good Witch is entirely true," Quinn said.

"Glad I'm on her side," Bo Ray said, and they all laughed.

"As far as finding you, I knew that Selena Duarte knew more than she was saying. I don't think she was even being all that elusive on purpose, even though she was scared and believed that the *rougarou* would leave her alone as long as she kept quiet." He shook his head. "Beauchamp actually made me really like him when we were with Selena. He reminded her that she'd die alone if she kept being so mean. I thought he cared about her. Now I realize that everything about his personality was a mask, just like the wolf's head mask he wore."

"How did he manage to rip out throats the way that he did?" Bo Ray asked.

"Novak did the throat ripping," Deerfield said. "He's had all his back teeth filed to a point. Beauchamp couldn't do it. There were a few times when he had to be in uniform quickly. So being covered in blood wouldn't work. Beauchamp told Jim Novak that honing his teeth was a way of preparing to be the *rougarou* himself."

They all sat in silence for a moment.

"Something scared the '*rougarou*' off the balcony when he came into the city. I'm sure he meant to take Jane Eagle and Lana Adair," Deerfield said.

"Probably someone in the street, or the fact that a scream would have drawn attention," Larue said. "Those girls don't know how lucky they are."

"But which one came into the city as a *rougarou*?" Natasha asked.

"It was actually Hayden Beauchamp that night," Larue said. "Which is probably why the girls are still alive. Beauchamp didn't want to get caught. Novak saw himself as a *rougarou* in training. I don't think he would have been scared away."

"Let's hope that they're both locked up forever," Natasha said.

"They could get the death penalty," Father Ryan said, which brought everyone there to look at him.

He lifted his hands. "Judgment isn't mine. I'm just referring to the law in the state of Louisiana."

A moment later, Quinn was asked up to play with the group, which he did. And it felt wonderful. It reminded him that he was alive. That they were alive.

Good times were what made up for the bad times. Now and then, Quinn glanced at the table. He was glad to see Danni smile at him. She was having fun. And she seemed to enjoy the fact that he was happy too. There was just something about a guitar, something soothing, even when his playing was really anything but. But he loved who he was playing with, loved the night. And loved that he had kept his word to Selena Duarte and the *rougarou* had been caught.

It was late when they all parted. Since Dirk Deerfield was still reeling, he was going to head out on vacation. That night, he was staying at Quinn's family home in the Garden District. The next morning he was flying off for a long awaited trip to London. They bid one another goodnight. Larue headed off in his car, as did Father Ryan and Deerfield. The rest of them piled into Quinn's car. They dropped Natasha off first, then parked in the garage at Danni's house on Royal Street.

Billie and Bo Ray headed up.

Danni and Quinn greeted Wolf and gave him treats.

Then Danni headed up.

Quinn checked the door to the basement. The items there had no power over anyone anymore, but Quinn still kept the basement door locked. He called to Wolf and they headed upstairs. The dog curled up in his bed. Quinn walked into the bedroom he shared with Danni.

She was waiting for him.

He smiled. "Maybe you are a witch. A temptress, driving men to madness, seducing them."

She frowned, rising to meet him. "Quinn, I've never been like that."

He laughed, taking her into his arms, loving the sensation of holding her, feeling her against him, especially with the image of her in the power of the "*rougarou*" still lurking in the back of his mind. For a moment, he held her tenderly. Then he caught her chin with his forefinger and lifted it.

"I mean nothing evil in that. Just teasing, my love. The cane is put away, far from the hands of those who might see it as an evil power. But your strength is entirely different and can't be shut away. You are a witch, of course, of the best kind. You have the kind of magic that seduced my heart and soul. With your laughter, your vitality, your concern for others in the world around you, and then of course—"

He paused.

"I love you for your—"

And he whispered in her ear.

"Ah," she said, drawing a finger gently down his cheek. "Let's make use of all that you love."

Her fingers then slid down the length of his back.

A good night lay ahead.

But he did want to know one thing. "Just how did you make it rain?"

"Magic," she said. "How else?"

* * * *

Also from 1001 Dark Nights and Heather Graham, discover Crimson Twilight, When Irish Eyes Are Haunting, and All Hallows Eve.

Sign up for the 1001 Dark Nights Newsletter
and be entered to win a Tiffany Key necklace.

There's a contest every month!

Go to www.1001DarkNights.com to subscribe.

As a bonus, all subscribers will receive a free
1001 Dark Nights story
The First Night
by Lexi Blake & M.J. Rose

Turn the page for a full list of the
1001 Dark Nights fabulous novellas...

Discover 1001 Dark Nights Collection Three

HIDDEN INK by Carrie Ann Ryan
A Montgomery Ink Novella

BLOOD ON THE BAYOU by Heather Graham
A Cafferty & Quinn Novella

SEARCHING FOR MINE by Jennifer Probst
A Searching For Novella

DANCE OF DESIRE by Christopher Rice

ROUGH RHYTHM by Tessa Bailey
A Made In Jersey Novella

DEVOTED by Lexi Blake
A Masters and Mercenaries Novella

Z by Larissa Ione
A Demonica Underworld Novella

FALLING UNDER YOU by Laurelin Paige
A Fixed Trilogy Novella

EASY FOR KEEPS by Kristen Proby
A Boudreaux Novella

UNCHAINED by Elisabeth Naughton
An Eternal Guardians Novella

HARD TO SERVE by Laura Kaye
A Hard Ink Novella

DRAGON FEVER by Donna Grant
A Dark Kings Novella

KAYDEN/SIMON by Alexandra Ivy/Laura Wright
A Bayou Heat Novella

STRUNG UP by Lorelei James
A Blacktop Cowboys® Novella

MIDNIGHT UNTAMED by Lara Adrian
A Midnight Breed Novella

TRICKED by Rebecca Zanetti
A Dark Protectors Novella

DIRTY WICKED by Shayla Black
A Wicked Lovers Novella

A SEDUCTIVE INVITATION by Lauren Blakely
A Seductive Nights New York Novella

SWEET SURRENDER by Liliana Hart
A MacKenzie Family Novella

For more information, visit www.1001DarkNights.com

Discover 1001 Dark Nights Collection One

FOREVER WICKED by Shayla Black
CRIMSON TWILIGHT by Heather Graham
CAPTURED IN SURRENDER by Liliana Hart
SILENT BITE: A SCANGUARDS WEDDING by Tina
Folsom
DUNGEON GAMES by Lexi Blake
AZAGOTH by Larissa Ione
NEED YOU NOW by Lisa Renee Jones
SHOW ME, BABY by Cherise Sinclair
ROPED IN by Lorelei James
TEMPTED BY MIDNIGHT by Lara Adrian
THE FLAME by Christopher Rice
CARESS OF DARKNESS by Julie Kenner

Also from 1001 Dark Nights

TAME ME by J. Kenner

For more information, visit www.1001DarkNights.com

Discover 1001 Dark Nights Collection Two

Also from 1001 Dark Nights

For more information, visit www.1001DarkNights.com

Discover more from Heather Graham

Crimson Twilight: A Krewe of Hunters Novella

It's a happy time for Sloan Trent and Jane Everett. What could be happier than the event of their wedding? Their Krewe friends will all be there and the event will take place in a medieval castle transported brick by brick to the New England coast. Everyone is festive and thrilled . . . until the priest turns up dead just hours before the nuptials. Jane and Sloan must find the truth behind the man and the murder--the secrets of the living and the dead--before they find themselves bound for eternity--not in wedded bliss but in the darkness of an historical wrong and their own brutal deaths.

When Irish Eyes Are Haunting: A Krewe of Hunters Novella

Devin Lyle and Craig Rockwell are back, this time to a haunted castle in Ireland where a banshee may have gone wild— or maybe there's a much more rational explanation—one that involves a disgruntled heir, murder, and mayhem, all with that sexy light touch Heather Graham has turned into her trademark style.

All Hallows Eve: A Krewe of Hunters Novella

Salem was a place near and dear to Jenny Duffy and Samuel Hall -- it was where they'd met on a strange and sinister case. They never dreamed that they'd be called back. That history could repeat itself in a most macabre and terrifying fashion. But, then again, it was Salem at Halloween. Seasoned Krewe members, they still find themselves facing the unspeakable horrors in a desperate race to save each other-and perhaps even their very souls.

For more information, visit www.1001DarkNights.com

On behalf of 1001 Dark Nights, Liz Berry and M.J. Rose would like to thank ~

Steve Berry
Doug Scofield
Kim Guidroz
Jillian Stein
InkSlinger PR
Dan Slater
Asha Hossain
Chris Graham
Pamela Jamison
Jessica Johns
Dylan Stockton
Richard Blake
BookTrib After Dark
The Dinner Party Show
and Simon Lipskar

Made in the USA
San Bernardino, CA
29 April 2016